TURN LEFT AT THE COW

Lisa Bullard

HOUGHTON MIFFLIN HARCOURT
Boston   New York

www.hmhbooks.com
Text set in Janson

Library of Congress Cataloging-in-Publication Data
Bullard, Lisa.
Turn left at the cow / Lisa Bullard.
pages cm
Summary: "Thirteen-year-old Trav feels like a fish out
of water in rural Minnesota in this coming-of-age mystery about a boy who discovers his dad may have been a
bank robber."—Provided by publisher.
ISBN 978-0-544-02900-2
[1. Fathers—Fiction. 2. Mystery and detective stories.
3. Minnesota—Fiction.] I. Title.
PZ7.B91245Tu 2013
[Fic]—dc23
2012047542

Manufactured in the United States of America
DOC 10 9 8 7 6 5 4 3 2 1
4500431208

For Vicki Liestman, who once changed my life by encouraging me to build a (metaphorical) barn.

CHAPTER 1

There were so many dead bodies stuffed into Gram's freezer chest that it was kind of like wandering through a cryonics lab. You know, one of those places where they turn rich old guys into Popsicles? Gram had been hearing odd noises from her cellar for a while now, and she was convinced it was this dying freezer she kept there. So my punishment for the day was to clean it out and stuff everything into these jack-o'-lantern leaf bags that Gram had been saving since who knows how many Halloweens ago.

In Grandma Land, even the contents of the freezer were way different than what I was used to. Agreeing on what a freezer should hold seemed to be the only thing my new stepfather and I had in common. But here, instead of meeting up with my best buds Ben and Jerry, I was finding Nemo and his friends, wrapped up in white packages with writing on the outside so you could clue into whichever member of the magical forest had taken a hit and when.

I stuffed "Duck" and then "Venison" and "Walleye" into another one of the pumpkin bags. Man, those packages had been waiting to be set free longer than I had. Maybe the noises Gram had been hearing weren't from the freezer. Maybe they were from the ghosts of all these dead things, plotting up some serious revenge.

By the time I reached the bottom of the frozen graveyard, Gram's cellar was feeling a lot like one of those the-killer-is-in-the-basement places, where the stupid kid always ends up kicking it in slasher movies. Only one big ice-covered box was left. I bent over the side of the freezer chest and tugged at the corner of the box. Not enough leverage—the thing was iced in place as if it had been Gorilla-Glued.

I hoisted my upper half deep into the chest and yanked again. No go. I leaned way over, hanging on to the edge of the freezer with one hand while I grabbed the box with the other. Then I got my Hulk on and gave one last mighty pull.

That's when Nemo and his friends finally took their revenge. Turned out the stupid box was heavier than I'd realized. I leaned too far and pulled too hard, and then the box broke free and I over-ended into the appliance of death.

As I was falling in, something rolled out of the box into the bottom of the freezer. The last thought I had before I landed on it was that maybe I had some mutant form of jet lag or something. Because I could have sworn it looked exactly like a head.

A frozen human head.

CHAPTER 2

The finale of my Olympic high-diving act into the freezer was the really macho yet graceful way I managed to contort my body so I didn't break my neck. Instead, I back-flopped hard enough that I knocked the wind out of myself. I was desperately trying to suck the air back into my lungs while simultaneously desperately trying not to think about The Thing that was now jabbing into my spine. Or about who might have stored it in the bottom of Gram's freezer.

A head. A frozen human head.

I had a pretty good idea who was responsible for the rest of the inhabitants of the deep freeze. Given the dates written on all of the white packages, it was most likely my dead-before-I-was-born father who had hunted down Bambi and Co. and then bundled them away, where they'd lain forgotten after my dad kicked the bucket himself.

But had he also been the kind of dude to stash human body parts in the backup appliance? Even though I'd spent all of yesterday's trip from California to Minnesota thinking through every question I had about him—all the things I was desperate to know, all the questions I was finally going to convince Gram to answer—I'd never thought to add "Am I the son of a psycho killer?" to the list.

Suddenly I heard an unfamiliar voice ask, "Where is he? Mrs. Stoiska said he was down here."

I made a weird wheezing sound as my body finally managed to haul in some oxygen. Two faces popped over the edge of the freezer chest and looked down at me.

"Dude!" said Face One. "We found you! You're Travis, right?" The kid sounded way excited; even Gram hadn't been that happy to see me.

"Trav," I croaked, peering up at him.

"Taking a little nighty-night?" asked Face Two. She didn't seem as pleased to meet me as Face One had; if I hadn't already been glacierized by my time in the freezer chest, I would have been totally iced by the cool dripping off her voice.

Thinking about being iced made me remember the other, unknown occupant of the chest, and I hurriedly hoisted myself to my feet. I scrambled over the side of the freezer and backed away for good measure.

"What were you doing in there?" asked the girl, still really cold. She looked to be about my age, so what was up with her evil fairy act, anyway?

"I was cleaning it out and this box got stuck and turns out it was a—ah . . ." I could hear my voice trailing off. I hadn't had time to think about what strategy the situation called for. Maybe it was better not to clue in the townsfolk until I'd had a chance to weigh the pros and cons of having Hannibal Lecter in the family.

But the girl had already figured out that something was going on, and she peered back into the dimly lit freezer. Then she straightened up and turned to the blond guy. He topped me by a few inches and he was built like a tank. But it was hard to imagine he could be much older than I was—thirteen—since he had the kind of bright-eyed look you usually only see on two-year-olds at the ice cream store.

"I think he found your mom's head," Evil Fairy said to him.

"Really?" said the Jolly Green Giant. "You mean she's been here the whole time?"

"Looks pretty good, too," said the girl.

"Lemme see," said the kid.

While they staged the family reunion, I inched my way toward the stairs. Were these the types of aliens who showed up to make crop circles? I wasn't sure, but this Old McDonald–ville town of Gram's was starting to seem like the kind of place where they would order pizza and then eat the delivery guy.

The girl turned to me. "I think you smooshed her nose."

I made a hands-up gesture to signal to the alien beings that I had come from California in peace.

Evil Fairy said to the giant, "He looks a little freaked, Kenny. Show him the head."

Kenny reached down into the freezer and, with an easy one-handed scoop, pulled up The Thing.

Once it was out of the freezer, I could tell instantly

that it wasn't real. I mean, if it hadn't been for all my thinking about dead things, I probably would have never made the mistake. But okay, so even if it wasn't real, who on earth kept fake human heads in their freezer? And what in the name of Sara Lee was the thing made out of, anyway?

Evil Fairy must have been able to read my mind, because she reached out and scraped a fingernail down the back of the head and then held her finger out toward me.

"Butter," she said.

"Butter?" I repeated. "Who makes a head out of butter?"

Kenny beamed and laughed a Jolly Green Giant mighty laugh. "My mom was Dairy Princess or something years ago at the state fair, and they carved her head out of butter. She got to take it home, but then at some point she forgot where she stored it, and it turned into one of those family jokes. You know? Where anytime somebody loses something, we're all, like, 'Maybe it's gone to be with the butter head.'"

I was still trying to play connect-the-dots with this story when Kenny tucked the butter head under his arm like he was going to run it in for a touchdown.

"I gotta show Mom. She'll be so happy you found it!" And he charged up the stairs and out the door, leaving me alone in the cellar with the ticked-off pixie.

Evil Fairy and I stood in silence until I couldn't take it anymore.

"Kenny seems real nice," I said. "And it's easy to see that he hangs with you because you're so much fun to have around."

She tossed her hair and marched toward me until she was standing really close, then she jabbed her hands onto her hips and leaned in.

"I know," she said, pretty much snarling, "that you're here to find the money your father stole from that bank. But you can just go back to La-La Land empty-handed, because Kenny and I are going to figure out where he hid the bank loot first."

Then she stomped up the stairs and out the door, leaving me alone with four pumpkin bags full of dead body parts and a whole new set of questions.

CHAPTER 3

Bagging up body parts was my punishment for showing too much initiative.

It doesn't seem fair that initiative turned out to be so punishment-worthy. I mean, that's all Ma ever talked about, how I should get off the couch and show some initiative, make some new friends if I was really that unhappy with our new home and new life. So yesterday, I initiated myself cross-country all the way from Southern California to the town in Minnesota where my dad had grown up and where Gram still lived. A place I'd never been allowed to visit before.

The reality was, I didn't actually have permission to travel the two thousand miles over the river and through the woods to Grandmother's house this time, either. But I was counting on the fact that once the deed was done, Ma would secretly be happy to have me out of her newly married hair for a while.

It turned out that those things teachers say about how someday you'll actually use the junk you learn in school — totally true. I took all my geography and persuasive speech and research skills and mixed them up into a math word problem, and I was across two time zones before any of the grownups in my life even knew that I'd left California.

First I had talked Ma into letting me stay home alone while she and Dale took this day trip they'd been yammering about for weeks. Then I jumped into action. I knew Ma's credit card number and every password she'd ever forgotten; it was easy to buy a plane ticket online. She could dock my allowance for the rest of my life if that was what it would take for me to pay her back, but I was going to make this trip. I packed a carryon and dug out the cash I'd been stashing in my sock drawer for months. I knew where Ma kept my birth certificate hidden, too; along with my school ID, the airline website said that was all I would need to get on the plane as a thirteen-year-old unaccompanied minor.

I texted Ma throughout the day to tell her everything was going fine at home. Meanwhile, one cab, one plane, two commuter trains, and one bus later, I was an hour away from Gram's house in Minnesota.

I called Gram, told her where I was, and asked if she'd come pick me up. She said she was leaving right that minute and that I needed to hang up my cell and call my mother immediately.

I probably could have heard Ma across those two time zones even without my phone. But the yelling wasn't anything new. I mean, when I was a little kid, things were great; we were this regular happy family, even though it was just the two of us. And even though it bugged her that I asked all these questions about my dad. She always said she'd tell me everything when I was older. But how old did you have to be to deserve the truth?

And then a while back she got together with Dale and somehow it was just the two of them, all lovey-dovey to the point that any reasonable person would seriously barf. And I was on the outside. By the time they got married this past Christmas and we moved all the way to Dale's house, I was just her annoying kid who refused to accept his new stepdad. But Dale wasn't a fair trade for giving up my friends, my school, and the place I still thought of as home.

She kept trying to pass it off as something she was doing for my sake because I had never had a dad. But I didn't want a replacement father. I wanted my real father to feel real.

So I took things into my own hands and came to see the place that my dad had thought of as home. Sure, I wasn't exactly thrilled to discover that he'd grown up in the middle of what seemed to be endless farm fields. An ocean or a mountain would have been a nice change of scenery. Still, I wasn't going to let the actual location matter, now that I was so close to getting the answers that Ma wouldn't give me.

When Gram pulled up at the bus shelter and got out of her old Ford pickup, she barely said hello. She just put her hand out for my cell phone and told me to go wait in the truck. Fifteen minutes later, she climbed into the driver's seat and handed me back my phone.

"Your mother has reluctantly agreed that you can stay for a while, as long as I punish you with daily work projects." Gram pulled away from the curb, and I felt a huge smile spread across my face. I'd done it.

Gram tightened her lips. "I think it would be

prudent, Travis, if you managed to convey the impression that you see this as a prison sentence, not a vacation." And then, I swear, she winked at me. Or maybe it was just a twitch, because she never cracked a smile.

Which was how I ended up spending my first morning in Minnesota cleaning out the freezer chest without complaining, even though Gram's house was actually a little lake cabin set just past the edge of the fields, so I should have been stretched out on her dock working on my almost-July tan instead.

And it was also how the evil fairy had managed to catch me with my guard down; I think that freezer of death was putting off some kind of toxic fumes that didn't mix well with jet lag or something.

"Travis?" Gram's voice floated down into the cellar.

"Here," I called, snapping alert. I hefted one of the bulging orange bags and hauled it up the steps, plunking it down at her feet. "There're still three more down there."

Gram raised her eyebrows. "There won't be enough room in the garbage can, and trash pickup isn't until next week. The raccoons will be setting up a party if we leave them out." She nodded toward her truck. "We better haul them away now."

Too bad. Compared to my social life since I'd moved into the stephouse, even a raccoon party sounded good. I loaded up the truck while Gram limped inside to get her purse and keys. Then we headed off down the road away from the lake. I stared out the window, wondering how a place this empty could still qualify as a state. How would GPS even work? "Turn left at the cow"?

After a short time we came across a few buildings and then a giant statue of this way ugly fish. I was still staring at it as we turned a corner, and suddenly we were back to the vast open green that spread far and flat to a distant overlap with the sky. In my part of California, only the ocean is allowed to stretch out like that.

The truth was, Gram and I hardly knew each other. She used to come visit me once a year out in California, but after Dale entered the picture, that stopped; she didn't seem to fit into my new steplife any better than I did. But I knew this about her: she wasn't one of those grownups who always needed to be poking at you with words just to suck up all the air space. So it was quiet in the truck.

Which gave me plenty of time to try to make sense out of what the evil fairy had said.

My dad had been a bank robber?

But instead of focusing on that, for some crazy reason I started obsessing about the ex-planet Pluto.

When I was a really little kid, I lived for all that space stuff. Ma had even pasted a glow-in-the-dark universe onto the ceiling of my room, back at our old house. Back when things were just the two of us. She'd let me and my best friend, Jason Kalooky, have sleepovers all the time, and we'd lie there, looking up at the ceiling and arguing about the best planet. Kalooky always picked Jupiter because he liked that it was the biggest. I always took Pluto. I got that it was small compared to Jupiter, but as far as I was concerned, it was one tough little ice planet.

Then the science guys took a vote, and all of a sudden Pluto wasn't a planet anymore. Ma explained that we were supposed to call it a *dwarf* planet. But after that, even though I wanted to still love Pluto, I couldn't. It wasn't a real planet anymore—it was like finding out that your favorite player was juiced when he hit all those home runs. Asterisk this in the record book of life: *You may think you can count on things, but you can't. They always let you down.*

What I mean is, I already knew all about life's little disappointments. So I probably shouldn't have been feeling like Luke Skywalker when he finds out that Darth Vader is his dad and screams "Nooooooooo!" and jumps down into that void. But somehow I couldn't help it. The evil fairy's words kept spinning in my head like one of those pinwheels. And there was this void where the floorboards of the old pickup should have been that was screaming out for me to jump.

Even if the evil fairy was right, my dad had been just a bank robber, not some asthmatic guy named Darth who wanted to rule the galaxy. But the dark side is the dark side no matter what star system you come from. And bank robber—that's the dark side. Maybe on the spectrum of evil, it doesn't beat psycho killer, but it definitely outranks litterbug. And I'm guessing Luke Skywalker and I could agree: you're never really ready to discover your dad is from the dark side.

Normally I'm Mr. Cool, so I think it was being all worked up over Pluto that made me suddenly blurt out, "Why didn't you tell me my dad was a bank robber?"

Gram's head whipped around and the truck veered toward a ditch. And a bunch of cows—yeah, real live cows—stopped chewing grass and looked at us over their fence. Gram straightened out the truck and then stared directly ahead, all focused, watching the road like it was about to transform into the Ventura Freeway at rush hour.

"Where did you hear that?" she finally asked.

Trust a grownup to stall by answering a question with another question. "I don't know her name," I said. "This girl. Straight dark hair. Pointy kind of face. Bad attitude. She was with a big blond kid named Kenny."

"Isabella," said Gram. "Kenny's cousin. Kenny lives next door. Isabella and her sister are staying there for now too." She finally glanced back my way. "I sent them down to the cellar to introduce themselves. I never imagined they'd bring up . . ."

"The deep, dark family secret everybody's kept hidden from me for thirteen years? I mean, why should I get to know? I'm only the *son* in this story. It's a good thing the neighbor's cousin knows, but let's make sure we keep old Trav out of the loop, right?"

I guess she could tell I was a little ticked, because I saw her take a deep breath and then let it out slowly before she answered. Ma used to do that with me, too. Now Ma just goes straight to ticked.

"You're right, Travis. When you turned up here so unexpectedly, I knew I would need to talk with you about this soon. I was just hoping to find the right way to do that before someone else . . ." Gram's lips kind of pulled in and then she said, "Can we please talk about it later? Is that okay? Can we wait until we're back home?"

I shrugged and turned to look out the window. No surprise. I was used to getting the brushoff from Ma when it came to the things that mattered to me. I pulled out my music and plugged in the ear buds. The truth was, all the tunes I'd loaded had really been bugging me lately; they were all wrong somehow, like listening to the soundtrack for a chick flick when you were watching a Jackie Chan movie. But I knew Ma hated it when I shut her out that way, and I figured it might work on Gram, too. So I turned up the volume and watched for more cows.

Suddenly the scenery wasn't so much Cowpoke Sam as it was that part of LA where you double-check your car locks as you drive through. And the smell—I mean, man, this was like a cross between the time I left half a pizza under my bed for a week and the "mystery meat" in the school cafeteria. I turned off the music and looked at Gram.

"What is this place?"

"The dump," said Gram. Huh. Apparently Minnesota did have a few hidden wonders.

We drove through a gate in a chainlink fence and pulled up to a stop sign. Somebody had put a second little sign below the regular red one that read TAKE TURNS. I looked around. Other than the cows, I wasn't sure who we were supposed to take turns with.

Gram moved forward up a ramp and then jerked to another stop. She got out of the truck and walked over to talk to this guy who had come out of a trailer. They started chatting and pointing, yakking about whatever it is you yak about with the dump guy.

Meanwhile, I checked out the rest of WALL-E World from the safety of the truck: door-less refrigerators and heaps of garbage mounded high. Gulls were dive-bombing into the piles, screaming like extras in a Hitchcock movie. There was a bulldozer sitting quiet and lonely, way over on the other side of the enclosure, but I didn't see the point—you would have to bull-doze 24/7 just to keep up.

The dump guy pointed one final time and Gram climbed back into the truck, bumping along in the direction he had sent us. We curved around a bathtub and stopped right past a mannequin standing up in a rusting-out freezer chest not so different than the one I'd done a header into earlier that morning. Gram motioned me out of the truck and began climbing out herself. A shadow caught my eye and I tipped my head back; low overhead, three big black birds with small red heads circled, their spread wings fanning across the blue sky.

Gram tipped her head back too. "Buzzards. Turkey vultures. They're drawn in by the smell of decay."

Excellent. Maybe tomorrow we could take a field trip to the funeral home.

Gram told me to jump up into the truck bed and throw down the trash bags. I was tossing the last one onto a heap when this guy rose up out of the garbage, really mad, yelling and swinging something around his head, like some kind of maniac karate master. I swear, he was about to storm the back of the truck; I scrambled backwards, tripped, and sat down hard in the truck bed. Then I heard Gram's voice.

"Carl! Carl, it's okay—this is my grandson, Travis."

The guy pretty much froze midair and then wilted down into himself. He looked like a bag of bones held together by a nasty pair of coveralls. He muttered something, giving me the evil eye from underneath matted hair that hung down into his face. Gram walked over and touched his arm, murmuring something to him. She reached into her purse and took out what looked like cash and handed it over. He gave me one last dirty look, then loped off.

"What's with him?" I stood and brushed off the back of my shorts, watching as the guy scrabbled up a pile of garbage bags and slid down the other side, out of sight.

"I'm sorry, Travis—he's a very ill old man." Gram sighed and turned back to the truck. "Let's go home."

Then, despite saying earlier that she wanted to wait to talk, as soon as we were moving again she started in, spacing out her words all careful and slow, like she was reading off a phone number and wanted to make sure I got it down right.

"I know I should have talked to you about all this before, but your mother didn't want me to, and I was too—" She stopped and cleared her throat. Gram was probably telling the truth about that; I was sure Ma had told her the "don't ask, don't tell" policy that applied to my old man.

Gram didn't look at me, didn't reach out to me—she just kept talking. "But there's no excuse for me letting you down. So . . . things weren't good for your father after he came home from the army. I spent months hoping he'd find his way to the next right thing, but it never seemed to happen. Sometimes he'd be better for a while, like when he met your mother. He was happy then. But things would get worse again."

She stopped and took a breath. I was sure I looked like one of those big clown-head garbage cans, my mouth hanging wide open and my eyes bugging out at this sudden release of information after all the years of silence.

"Overall his life was going downhill. He couldn't hold on to a job, and your mother eventually left for California without him, a few months before you were born. Then one morning, the old deputy knocked on my door and asked if he could come in. He said, 'Mrs.

Stoiska, I've got some difficult news, ma'am.'" Gram finally looked over at me. "It had been a stormy night; your father's boat had been found washed up onshore over on the other side of the lake, and there was no sign of him.

"I called your mother. She hadn't heard from him. I didn't hear from him either. A few weeks later, men in dark jackets turned up. The FBI. They said that someone had stolen a lot of money from a bank in this small town up north, just before your father vanished. For some reason they were convinced your father had something to do with it. They searched his house. But they never found the money. And they never found him. I never saw him again."

Gram stared out the bug-guts-plastered windshield. She was gripping the steering wheel so hard that her knuckles stuck up like white bones, even though we had been parked in her driveway for the past five minutes.

Suddenly somebody knocked on the passenger-side window. I jumped and turned my head away from Gram to look. It was Kenny—and Isabella. "Hey, Butter Head," he said, smiling real big. "Me and Iz are going out fishing in my boat—wanna come?"

CHAPTER 4

I stood there, holding a clean T-shirt, seriously thinking about going AWOL out my bedroom window. The invitation to the fishing trip had hardly been out of Kenny's mouth before Gram was gushing away, saying "doesn't that sound like fun" and all but carrying me down to the boat herself. She made it pretty clear I was heading out to catch me a big one, like it or not. My guess was she needed some alone time and couldn't figure out how else to get rid of me.

And grownups—they always assume that just because you're the same age as somebody, you'll be best buds in minutes. But it wasn't hard to tell that one wrong move on my part, and Isabella—Iz?—might sprinkle me with evil fairy dust.

The problem was, a whole long list of possible

wrong moves on my part seemed inevitable, since my hands-on experience with fish began when they were already in the fish sticks stage. Ma wasn't exactly the bait-your-hook type. And since my father had disappeared sometime after his close encounter of the biological kind with her, but before I squirted into the world, I never had that Family Channel moment where my daddy taught me how to fish. Looking stupid on a fishing trip with the kids next door just wasn't at the top of my wish list.

Besides, the last thing I really wanted to see right now was a fish. After less than a day in Minnesota, I felt like I was drowning in some pretty deep stuff. And the truth was, it was a fish that had given me the dumb idea to run away from home in the first place.

See, there is this certain kind of catfish that can actually wiggle out of its pond and walk around on land until it finds a better place to rest its little fishy head. It lives in Asia, I think, or maybe it's Florida. But the point is, it's a real fish, and it really walks. I swear— you can catch it on Animal Planet if you don't believe me. Anyway, one night when the rest of California was nestled all snug in their beds, I saw it on cable and decided this fish was onto something.

Because if its pond dries up, or if it gets tired of it, then this catfish just up and boogies on to the next pond over. So I started thinking about my own pond and how much it didn't feel like home, and next thing I knew, I was making plans to get out of there—to shimmy my way cross-country to a different pond.

A pond where I could maybe figure out who my real dad had been instead of dealing with this step-father Ma was so eager to have me adopt. After all, there was a whole other half to my gene pool that I'd never been given the chance to swim in.

Except somehow I'd thought this would turn out to be some Disney movie, and now it was looking more like something rated R, like I was in over my head.

But no matter how I felt about fish, right then I just couldn't deal with sitting at home, trying to figure out what I was supposed to say to Gram. Putting my-self into a situation where I was bound to look like a total dork seemed like the better option.

Kenny and Iz were waiting in this little red old-fashioned fishing boat by the dock next door to Gram's. Iz pointed me to the bench seat between where she was sitting up front and where Kenny was sitting in back running the motor. We bounced across the waves for a while without saying anything. Kenny steered us close to this island that was a ways offshore, then cut back on the power. The motor started hacking like some three-packs-a-day geezer.

"We brought food if you're hungry." Iz waved toward some white paper bags sitting on the seat next to me. My insides were squeezing together, reminding me that I hadn't had anything to eat since breakfast. I grabbed the nearest bag; inside was a small Styrofoam container. I pried open the lid. It held a mysterious substance that Minnesotans apparently considered food, but this looked even stranger than the "Tater Tot hotdish" Gram had served at dinner the night before. Actually, it looked like something you'd find Orange County housewives nibbling on: some kind of rain forest granola made of grass shavings and—what were those white balls—maybe some kind of spiral pasta?

Suddenly one of the spirals moved. It uncurled and stretched itself toward the sun. I shrieked and threw the container up into the air. Small white balls began unwinding all across the bottom of the boat. One tickled my left foot. A seagull wheeled low overhead and screamed like a two-year-old. I was pretty sure that was exactly how I had sounded a few seconds before.

"Dude?" Kenny grinned. He had gotten the motor under control. "Hey, when you're done with your snack, hand me that other bag, the one with the cookies, okay?"

"Coordinated much?" Iz smirked as she pulled one of the spirals out of her hair. But then she hunkered down and started picking up the grubs or whatever they were off the bottom of the boat, tossing them back into the Styrofoam container. "They'll dry out if we don't get them back under cover pretty quick," she said as I joined her. "And then you two won't have any bait."

"You're not fishing?" I asked, relieved that the conversation had moved so quickly to any topic other than my clearly unbalanced mental state.

She gave me a sideways look. "I'm fishing for something . . . else." She dropped the carton onto the bench next to me and returned to her seat.

Kenny handed me a fishing pole. I let him have first go at the container of bait while I pretended to make a show of examining the pole. Really I was watching to see exactly how he got the squirmy little bugger onto the hook.

After only a couple of grub-gut squirts onto my

shorts, I got my hook baited and my line into the water. Kenny kept the boat crawling along, running parallel to the curve of the island. Iz had taken out some kind of electronic device and was peering into a screen.

"Wii Fisherperson?" I said. "GPS, in case we lose track of shore?" That was a laugh. There was no place you could go on this lake where you could lose track of shore; it was a kiddie pool compared to the big bad Pacific I was used to.

Iz jerked her shoulders without looking up.

"We borrowed Uncle Butch's underwater camera," Kenny said. "He uses it as a fish finder. But Iz is looking for"—he paused and reeled his line in a bit —"not fish," he finally said.

I had always been good at fill-in-the-blank tests, and I was starting to get a strange idea about what we might be fishing for. I turned to Iz. "You're using the underwater camera to look for . . . ?"

She finally lifted her big storm-cloud eyes and stared at me. "Some people think maybe your father— and the stolen money, too—ended up on the bottom of the lake. I'm sorry if you don't want to think about it. But I have to find that money. And we invited you along because after this morning, Kenny convinced me we need your help."

I stared out over the side of the boat. Even as close as we were to the island, you couldn't see the bottom of the lake; the low-running waves kept washing away the lake's secrets. Sunbeams ricocheted off the water in all directions like bullets of light. The gulls had settled back onto the waves and were bouncing up and down, looking just like bobble heads.

Iz thought that the lake might hold part of the answers I needed.

Finally I looked back at her. "Gram confirmed that there's a Wanted poster out there with my dad's picture on it. But I'm guessing there's a whole lot more to the story than she's already told me. So maybe you better go ahead and catch me up on everything you know."

CHAPTER 5

Kenny just kept tossing his line into the water. Iz was the chatty one. "Here's the way everybody figures it: Your father robbed that bank up north. Then he came back to town to hide the money. Then he drowned. So the money has to still be around here somewhere, right? I mean, the cops never found any of it."

I thought her theory had more holes than my old gym socks, but before I could ask any questions, Kenny suddenly clapped a hand to his forehead. "What time is it? I promised Mom we'd be home by two fifteen to babysit the brats."

Iz looked at her watch. "So sad. Yet again you've messed up. It's two thirty."

"I wouldn't celebrate so fast. You're supposed to have been there too, Miss Perfect. This is why I need a cell phone." Kenny was reeling in his line double time.

Iz snorted. "Well, if you hadn't put your first one through the wash and dropped the second one in the lake . . ."

"You can borrow mine." I pulled it out of my pocket and handed it over.

"Whoa, is this sweet or what?" Kenny turned my phone over in his hands. "My friend Cody has one just like it. He says you can practically program it to launch a nuclear missile attack in between texts."

I have to admit, I was pretty proud that I had technology to rival Bill Gates, but Iz rolled her eyes and sighed bigtime while I showed Kenny some of the phone's best features.

"Uh—two thirty-four?" she said, tapping her watch.

Kenny hurriedly dialed and had one of those conversations where the other person—his mom, I guessed—doesn't let you finish a sentence. All he could squeeze in was "But we" and "But I" and a sad little "All right" before he hung up.

"Hang on." He looked at us, then revved up the motor and bounced us back over the waves with enough speed that at one point I thought I was going to involuntarily donate a kidney to one of the gulls flying overhead.

Gram managed to avoid me as much as possible for the rest of the day. I guess she'd used up her quota of words and wasn't ready to do any more gut spilling. So it was a relief when Kenny called later that night to say the baby-sitting gig had wrapped and I should come by for an after-dark swim.

Five minutes later I was standing on his dock in my swim shorts, watching the moon rise up yellow and lopsided over the dark lake.

"I tested the water this afternoon, man, and it was pretty cold," I said.

"Don't be such a baby." Iz tossed her head. "The ice has been out for two months now." She lowered her voice. "The little kids will come pester us if we sit on the dock. Nobody will bother us if we're out on the raft."

I could see Kenny's grin in the dark. "But to get there, you've got to risk freezing, California."

"At least here you don't have to worry about sharks," I muttered.

Kenny snickered. "Oh, we got Jaws here too, man.

Only this is a snapping turtle. Weighs in at about forty pounds. Just one snap and he can take off a guy's—"

"Kenny!" said Iz.

"A guy's *thumb*," finished Kenny.

This "why not go to Minnesota" idea of mine just kept getting better and better. I stood there for a minute, looking down at the cold, black water and thinking a little bit about Jaws and a little bit about my father and a little bit about the fact that Iz was wearing a swimsuit and standing right next to me in the dark.

Then something slammed into me and I went flipping through the air.

I hit the water with a smack and sank under. The cold sucked all the bones out of my body. Somehow I got my head up above the surface and spit out a lungful of lake. I could see Kenny's white smile again, floating next to me, and a sleek form sliding like a seal under the water past him. Iz.

"Only way to do it," said Kenny. "If you think too hard, you'll never go in." I had kind of gotten the impression that thinking too hard was never Kenny's problem, but it seemed the boy knew how to get things done when necessary. Something to remember.

We struck out for the raft and hoisted ourselves up

the side. We all lay back and looked up at the night. I was starting to understand why UFOs usually land in cow pastures; apparently you're a whole lot closer to the stars when you're out in the boonies.

"Where was I, in the story about your dad?" asked Iz. Her voice floated up next to me, really close in the dark. Goose bumps rose along my skin.

"You had just told me that the cops never found any of the money," I said.

"Right," she said. "But the guy who found your father's boat adrift remembered later on that there were big smears of clay all over the inside of it. The kind of clay that's under the topsoil around here."

"And that means . . . ?" I asked.

"Maybe your father had been digging somewhere. And the night your dad drowned, there was this really big storm. So people started asking, what would be important enough to make your father go out on the water in such bad weather? And all the old guys our fathers' age, they used to camp out on the island all the time when they were kids, so it was a place your dad knew really well. Everybody started thinking maybe your father decided to bury the money on the island."

"Okay, but this bank robbery—this all happened, like, before we were even born, right? How do you even know all this?"

"People talk about the robbery all the time. We've been listening to these stories our whole lives," said Kenny. "The big thing to do on a Sunday afternoon is to boat over and have a picnic with tuna sandwiches and watermelon and dig for the money. Whole island's probably been dug up about ten times over by now."

Yeah, forget what I said about the raccoon parties being a hot time here. Not when you've got tuna sandwiches and an island to dig up.

"And then some people figure your father could have gone overboard before he ever reached the island. So maybe the money went with him into the lake. Since nobody's ever found it," added Iz.

"When you say 'gone overboard,' you mean . . ." I wasn't sure how to finish.

I could hear Iz take a deep breath. "Well, maybe he fell overboard by accident in the storm. But my uncle says your father was a good swimmer. And the body never floated up or anything. Some people, they think he might have started to feel bad about what he'd done, so he went overboard more . . . on purpose. Like with an anchor tied around his foot."

I decided I wasn't really ready to think too much about the townsfolk's version of my father's plan B, so I steered the conversation back toward the money angle. "And you think you're somehow going to find the money even though the whole town's come up with nothing all these years. And then once you find it, the bank's going to let you keep it?" I could feel my voice rising up against the night.

Iz shifted and sat up next to me, and Kenny jumped into the conversation really fast. "It was in all the papers: after the robbery, the bank announced this big reward."

I had a lot of what seemed like really obvious questions. I wanted to ask Iz why she wanted the money so badly; I mean, it seemed as if this had to be about more than just a trip to the megamall. I wanted to ask them what if everybody was wrong, and my father never had anything to do with the bank robbery? I wanted to ask why nobody had ever considered that maybe my old man had just let the boat drift as a decoy and run off with all that cold hard "who wants to be a millionaire" cash in a suitcase. I mean, who was to say he wasn't actually still alive today and sitting on some tropical island somewhere, drinking out of one of those little glasses with an umbrella?

And I wanted to ask, *What happens if we do stumble across a bunch of bones that used to be Gram's only kid?*

But something told me to save those questions for another time.

"Okay, then," I said. "I get that you want to find the money. But what I don't get is why you think I can help you. Today is the first I'm hearing about any of this."

Iz leaned back onto her elbows. Kenny let out a breath.

"There was a whole day between when the bank was robbed and when they found the boat adrift and discovered your father was missing," Iz said. "Everybody remembers him hanging around town like usual that day in between. I got to thinking that maybe your father wrote a note. Or made a treasure map. He had plenty of time for it. When he didn't turn up later, your grandma cleaned out his house. Carried all his things home with her."

"The cops never found anything in his stuff. But maybe they didn't know what they were looking for. If your dad did make a map, maybe your grandma's got it now," said Kenny. "All we have to do is find it. And you're on the inside, man. We need your help."

The raft was shifting back and forth, back and forth, like a rocking chair under my back. I felt this big sigh heaving itself out of my body; my chest had gotten too tight, and the air needed to escape.

Iz said, "You'll help us, won't you?"

I watched one lone star hurtle across the sky and die over the edge of the horizon. Then I said the first thing that popped into my head. "I was thinking this morning about how they sent Pluto down to the minors so it didn't get to be a real planet anymore. Do you remember that? When we were just little kids? I took it kind of hard for some reason."

There was dead silence for a minute except for the sound of little waves licking at the raft's sides, and then Kenny said, "Yeah, I kinda remember that. I don't remember it being such a big deal, though."

"It's stupid, I guess, but I really loved Pluto. For a long time I kept hoping and hoping they'd put it back in the lineup, and then I finally gave up on it."

We all stared up at those huge honking stars for a while, and then Iz said, real quiet, "Because you figured out life just doesn't work that way. I get that." I turned my head to look at her and she looked over at me, and just for a second, it seemed as if her eyes had trapped some of those too-big stars. Then she shifted and the light flew back up into the night.

I wanted to believe in Pluto again, but Iz was right: life just doesn't work that way.

"Okay," I said, "I'm in. We're looking for a treasure map. And my father's bones. Where do we start?"

CHAPTER 6

When I was a really little kid, Ma was always spelling things over my head. I learned pretty fast that as soon as she started rattling off random ABCs, something big was going down. But I couldn't crack the alphabet code. So first there'd be the jumble of letters, and then I'd find myself being held down while the nice doctor gave me a shot.

Once I was halfway through first grade, she couldn't get away with spelling stuff, but she still worked really hard to keep me out of certain conversations. And back then I actually had a lot to say to her, so it really bugged me when she gave me the brushoff.

Which made it pretty funny that things turned around the way they did. Suddenly one day I wasn't so interested in talking to Ma. It was as if all those times I'd been shooed away had cured me of it. And as soon as that happened, Ma was wild to talk to me. All the time. She hammered at me about every last detail, asking about my new school and any new friends. Me, I just learned this look: I'd let my mouth hang open and my eyes glaze over, and I wouldn't answer anything until she said, "PAY ATTENTION to me when I'm talking to you," and I'd say, "Huh?" all innocent-like, and it would send her into a frenzy. Maybe she should have looked ahead and seen this coming when she was doing all that spelling.

The problem was, Gram wasn't anything like Ma. She was the queen of keeping things to herself; she hardly talked at all. Maybe it was from living alone for so long. But whatever the reason—I really needed her to start in with the gabbing a little more. Partly so somebody else's voice would interrupt all the spinning around my own thoughts were doing. Partly because I still had a lot of questions about dear Daddy-O and I needed them answered.

But now, on top of all that, I'd been given this secret mission. The America's Most Wanted neighborhood tag team wanted me to figure out if Gram held any clues to the missing money. Not exactly the easiest assignment in the world.

At breakfast the next morning, I studied Gram out of the corner of my eye. But with this invisible wall of silence between us, I had no idea how to get a conversation going that went further than "please pass the syrup." And it was a big leap from Aunt Jemima to "did you happen to find a treasure map with a big red X when you were cleaning out Dad's house after he disappeared?" So I just ate my pancakes and acted as if nothing else was going on, hoping to get my superhero invisible-wall-of-silence penetrating powers back online soon.

The pancakes were really good, though. I could have eaten, like, fifty of them.

Finally Gram spoke up. "I'd like you to come down to the church with me after breakfast. We're having a big fundraiser tomorrow night, and we could use your help setting some things up this morning. And Travis, you're dripping syrup on your shirt."

I had been so busy thinking about how to get Gram talking that when she actually started in, I stopped dead with this big bite halfway to my mouth and just held it there like a dork.

"Uh—okay." I made a bigger mess of the syrup on my shirt by scrubbing at it with my napkin. "But afterward, do you think I could hang out with Kenny and Iz? They wanted to take me out to the island this afternoon."

Gram took a long drink of coffee and set down her mug. "I imagine you'll have earned the right to some fun at that point. But I don't know exactly when I'll be able to leave the church to bring you home. Maybe . . ." She nodded over toward the back door, where a really strange-looking wooden cutout of a fish was hanging on the wall. A bunch of different-size keys hung off fishing hooks that were stuck to it.

"See that little gold key on the blue key chain? That's for the garden shed out in the yard. Somewhere buried in the back of it you should be able to find your father's old bike. He left it there when he moved out."

I jumped up and hurried over to the key rack. You'd never find anything like it on the wall in my stepfather's house. I mean, this fish just didn't look right, man; it was kind of lopsided and deformed and you could tell it wasn't that way on purpose, like when something's supposed to be Art. I hoped it wasn't based on some real fish; if there was a fish out there that looked like that, then the global warming dudes were right—the toxins were taking over and we all just better get in line behind the dodos and the polar bears.

Gram came up behind me. "Your father made that in junior-high shop class. Right when he was about your age. He was so proud that Christmas—he could hardly wait for me to open it."

She reached out with her bent-up old-lady finger and softly ran it across one edge, where the wooden fish had a big ragged lump sticking out. "He was upset when the shop teacher marked down his grade for not finishing this off. But John was always in a hurry to move on to the next thing life had to offer. What's one little rough spot when all the wide world is just waiting for you to jump in?"

She gave me a smile that somehow managed to be as sad as if she were bawling. "Of course, I told him the lump was my favorite part; I said it gave the whole piece character."

She plucked the gold key off the hook and handed

it to me. "As he got older, his rough spots kept getting rougher. I'm so sorry that his last jump landed him in a place where he never got to meet you, Travis. It's not what I would have wanted for either one of you."

I clutched the key in my fist. "I'll look for that bike," I muttered, and pretty much ran out the door. I guess that's what happens when grownups finally decide to start talking to you. They tell you stuff that just makes you feel worse about the rough spots in your own life.

Of course the bike wasn't there. So next thing I knew, we were back in the truck, heading to town to buy me a new bike, while I wondered how the morning had turned into one of those sitcoms from the olden days where the biggest problem in some kid's life is new braces or a bad math grade—or no bike.

Gram pulled over and parked on the side of the road. "Here we are. Come along, Travis."

I peered around while Gram climbed out of the truck. She had said we were going to town, so I had been watching for, well, a town.

This was, like, a block. I mean, there were those few buildings we'd passed going to the dump the day before. And one stop sign. And that giant fish statue. But I was still looking around, trying to figure it out, when I suddenly got it. This was it. All of it.

Gram went marching (as much as somebody with a limp can march) into a building that had—wait for it—a sign over the door saying THE BIG STORE. I guess when you could fit the whole town onto one block, then you could fit everything you needed into one store. We paused in front of some cow-size plastic animals that had trees or something growing out of their heads and looked around. Then Gram spotted bikes back behind a big display of pooper-scoopers.

"What do you think?" she asked, pointing to a black bike.

She had this excited "it's your birthday" look on her face. It told me that the Big Store was selling Trav a bike today even if there was an earthquake in the next five seconds. But I was pretty sure Gram wasn't exactly rolling in the dough. She drove an old beater and her furniture was all faded and I think maybe there were still dinosaurs around when she bought her TV. So I kind of pretended to be all interested in the pooper-scoopers while really I was trying to get a look at the price tag without Gram's noticing.

"Um—you know, Gram, you don't have to buy it for me. I mean, it's a great bike, but I can buy my own bike. I mean, I can pay you back later. I have a bunch of money in my room." And I did too. Not that I'm saying that made me special or anything, but it was true. My stepfather seemed to think he could buy my acceptance if he just threw enough cash my way.

Gram gave me a funny look. "That's very . . . manly of you, Travis, to want to pay for it yourself. I guess you really are growing up. But I won't be denied the pleasure of buying my grandson a bike. Try it out."

A guy in a green vest popped up while I was giving the bike the once-over. I noticed that his vest had THE BIG STORE "KING" stitched across the front. I wasn't sure why His Majesty had it in for me, but he was giving me the kind of look the substitute teacher gives the class when she's had her back turned and somebody rips a big one. It was starting to seem as if most of the people I met around here were ready to hate me on sight.

Gram turned to him. "Milo, you've never met my grandson, have you? Travis, this is Mr. Svengrud. He used to be on the football team with your father."

It was clear the King wanted to drop-kick me right

on out of there, but I guess he figured he couldn't actually injure a customer without a fat lawsuit on his hands.

Gram asked a bunch of questions about the bike, and the King was stuck having to answer them even though he still had that "who farted?" look on his face. At least it wasn't some dork-mobile ride or anything, which certainly wasn't a given in this town, considering that just across from the bikes was a rack of T-shirts that said "Minnesota: Home of the Loon-atics."

Gram finally said, "We'll take it." There was a moment when I thought the King was going to grab it away instead of letting us leave with it, but then he shoved it at me and stomped off. Gram watched him go, shaking her head with her eyebrows raised high, as if they were going to fly right off her forehead.

She turned and slipped me a big wad of cash from her purse. She lowered her voice. "You go ahead and pay for the bike yourself like you wanted to—nobody else has to know I gave you the money. I'm going to go pick up some charcoal." She limped away, all happy and pleased with herself, leaving me with nothing to do but roll the thing up to the front of the store and get in line to buy it.

But then I saw—or smelled, really—who was ahead of me. It was that crazy old guy who'd tried to take me down the day before at the dump. I started to pull back, but he jerked his head up all of a sudden and saw me.

He looked me over for a minute, and then his eyes got narrow and he moved in really close. "You're one of them aliens, ain't you?" he said, breathing on me with his dead-fish breath. "I've seen your kind falling from your spaceships into the lake at night." His claw-hand came up and gripped my arm, hard. "I'm on to you, space man."

"Carl!" Gram's voice spoke up behind me and he backed away fast, turning to throw a bunch of money onto the counter and grabbing up a couple of big bags. Then he gave me one last dirty look and took off out the door.

I wondered if he'd just paid for his stuff with the same money I'd seen Gram slipping him the day before; he didn't smell like somebody who held down a regular nine-to-five job.

Gram wasn't looking so happy anymore. I paid and we wheeled the bike outside. And the whole time, I kept thinking how ticked I was at Crazy Carl. I mean, it wasn't that I cared about him hating on me or anything, but I was feeling really bad that he'd managed to dump all over Gram's good mood.

She didn't say anything until I'd finished loading the bike into the back of the truck. "I'm not sure what to tell you about Carl, Travis. He wasn't always like this."

She paused and rubbed her hand along a scratch in the truck's paint. "Your father was just a little boy when your grandfather died in the car accident." She reached down and rubbed her leg. "The same accident where I acquired this limp. Carl was a buddy of your grandfather's, and he stepped in and took on a fatherly role with John, while I was recovering and afterward. I was so grateful for that—John was a boy who really needed a good man in his life, and Carl was certainly there for him when he was a little guy. He took him fishing and later hunting, taught him something about construction. Then, as your father got older, it was clear Carl was having some problems—but things really went downhill for him after John disappeared."

She looked over at the giant fish statue and shook her head. "In all these years, whatever his problems, I've never known Carl to hurt a flea. I can't imagine why he's taken such a dislike to you. Maybe you remind him too much of your father and it's stirred up hard memories for him. I guess you should stay out of his way as much as you can."

Like that wasn't already my plan.

But I was tired of talking about Crazy Carl, and I really wanted to put the happy-birthday look back onto Gram's face. So I gestured at the bike. "Thank you. It's a really great bike. I love it."

And there she went, smiling this big face-splitter. Then we both just stood there looking at each other while the thank-you-hug moment passed us by, because even when I saw her when I was little, she was never a start-it-off hugger. Back then, I had always hugged first and it always seemed to take her by surprise. Maybe I should have gone ahead and tried it again now, but I had given up on hugging altogether a while back.

Gram's watch alarm suddenly chirped, and we both jumped a little. "Oh, I said we'd be at the church by now. Travis, would you run across the street to the grocery store? Go to the deli counter and tell them you're picking up the big order for the church fundraiser." She handed me another wad of cash. "I'll go pick up the order at the bakery and meet you here at the truck."

Of course, that wasn't as easy as it sounded, because Crazy Carl had worked his way over to the grocery store. I mean, it wasn't like I was scared of him or anything—I just didn't need any more of the dude's aggravation. So after I got the stuff for Gram, I stood behind this big pyramid built out of cans of baked beans over by the checkout, where I could hang and watch, all nonchalantly, until I saw Crazy Carl leave the store.

Then suddenly I felt a hand on my shoulder from behind. And of course my reflexes took over, and I wheeled around and my foot kind of kicked out, and next thing I knew, bean cans were flying everywhere and rolling down two aisles. One knocked over this little kid like a bowling pin. He started howling, and his mother gave me The Look before she went to scoop him up.

And turns out it was just this guy in a store apron behind me. He was shaking his head and saying, "I was going to ask if I could help you find anything, son, but I see you've already located our bean selection."

I helped Apron Guy rebuild the can pyramid, my face feeling hot enough to toast marshmallows, while this really pretty high school checkout girl laughed her face off the whole time.

So even though the church was just down at the end of the next block, we were really late showing up. And I guess that was a big deal, because as soon as we walked into this big room in the basement, a whole group of old ladies charged over, saying stuff like, "Oh, we couldn't imagine what happened—you're always on time for everything, Lois," as they closed in around us like a pack going in for the kill. And even though they were all talking to Gram, they were really staring at me the whole time.

Which, I gotta say, was a little bit freaky. I mean, I just wasn't used to all those old people in one place. Where I live in California, we pretty much don't have any old-timers. I don't know what happens to them, but it's as if they don't let people back in through the gates once their hair turns gray.

"Ladies, I'd like to present my grandson, Travis," said Gram. "He's here on a little visit from California. Travis, the people in town call us the Church Ladies."

She took me around the circle, and each Church Lady shook my hand as Gram said everyone's name, all of them nodding and smiling at me as we worked our way one by one until it was as if we'd set loose a room full of wrinkly bobble heads.

No way I was going to remember the names of all of Gram's posse, so I spent the next couple hours "yes ma'am"–ing, hauling folding chairs, clanking down tables, and being polite while they all told me the Christmas-letter versions of their grandkids' lives. I had been thinking that maybe keeping your thoughts to yourself was an old-lady thing in general, but it turned out that it was mostly just a Gram thing. The rest of the posse chattered more than the Gossip Girls' table in the school cafeteria, their voices bouncing off the whitewashed cement walls so it sounded as if they'd multiplied themselves since we'd shown up.

But it wasn't so bad, really, until one of them suddenly put her hands onto her hips and looked me up and down. "I just can't get over how much you look like your father!"

And of course that was the exact moment when the room happened to be quiet. They all turned to stare at me again and started in on that nodding thing again too, until Gram limped over and said, "I think you've earned your freedom, Travis," and they scurried away.

"You worked hard today. Thank you," Gram said, reaching out to hand me another couple of bills from her purse. "Stop in town and buy yourself some lunch. Be careful when you go out to the island. I'll be home soon." Then she squeezed my arm, right where Crazy Carl had squeezed. It really hurt, but I didn't let her know that. "You're a good boy," she said, and walked away while I rubbed my arm and stared after her.

CHAPTER 7

I debated just zooming right through town, considering I'd had more than my share of strangers staring at me, but the pancakes seemed to have disappeared years ago. So I got three burgers to go from the café. I was about to buy a soda from the vending machine outside the gas station, but then I got closer and realized what it was.

Live bait. The machine actually sold live bait. What did it say about my life that I had willingly traded in California for a town where the vending machines sold worms?

So I went into the gas station, got my cold caffeine fix, and then hit the road again, sucking it all down as I pedaled past the green-striped fields back to Gram's. The church-basement smell of old ladies had cleared away and I was feeling pretty good. Until I saw Iz, sitting all folded around herself in Gram's yard. My stomach did this major flip-flop, and for a minute I was afraid I was going to hurl, but then everything settled down. Guess they're right that you should never drink and ride.

I wasn't sure if my guts were jumping because seeing Iz made me flash back to lying next to her on the raft the night before, or if it was because seeing her reminded me all over again about the bank-robber thing.

"Did you ask your grandma if she still had any of your dad's stuff so you could look through it?" She had this eager look on her face, so I squatted down and pretended to be really interested in some ants scurrying around a mega-anthill in the grass.

"Uh—didn't get a chance yet," I said.

Iz sighed real loud. "But last night you said you would—"

"Heads up!" I heard a voice yell. I looked up, grateful for the interruption, just in time to see a football arrowing directly for me. I barely managed to get my hands up to deflect it before it would have knocked me back. Kenny trotted over and looked at me sadly.

"You're supposed to *grab* it, not hide from it." He picked up the football, tossed it into the air, and caught it one-handed.

Iz unfolded and stood up in one smooth motion, reaching out to try and snag the ball from him. "Island time—say bye-bye to your baby, Kenny."

Kenny grumbled and stuck out his lip like he was going to argue, but Iz fisted her hands on her hips and he finally set the football down with a little pat on its leathered side. I hoped he'd keep on moaning; in the process of prodding him along, Iz seemed to have forgotten my broken promise about talking to Gram. We walked around to the lake side of the house, over to Kenny's dock, and loaded into his boat while Kenny continued to mumble under his breath.

The island wasn't that far out. We were halfway there, bouncing over seagull surf, when I realized something was missing. "No shovels?" I asked. "I thought the point of going out here was to dig for buried treasure."

Iz shook her head. "It's like Kenny told you yesterday—people have turned over the entire island ten times in the past few years. We're not going to waste our energy on that—we're going to look for land-marks," she said.

"Landmarks? You mean like a rock with an arrow painted on it pointing to a cave door?" I went on to point like a hunting dog and did my best Scooby-Doo imitation for her. "Look, it's a clue."

Kenny snickered, but Iz's dark eyebrows narrowed over her eyes in a way that told me I'd better tread carefully.

"No, dipwad, I mean I want you to walk around a little bit and check things out. That way, if you ever do get up the courage to ask your grandma about looking through your dad's things, you'll recognize a map of the island if you see one. Get it now?"

"Mood swings ahead—hold on to your life jack-ets, mateys," said Kenny. Iz transferred her scowl to him but Kenny just grinned back.

"I'm still a little confused," I said hurriedly, before Iz got it into her head to stage a mutiny. "I guess it just doesn't make sense to me. Tell me again why every-body in town is convinced this money is stashed on the island somewhere."

Iz put on that I-better-not-have-to-say-this-again

voice that Ma used sometimes. "Why else would your dad be out on the lake on such a stormy night other than to bury the money before the cops showed up?" She swept her arm through the air, waving it across the stretch of island.

Suddenly Kenny called out, "Little help here, Iz!"

We were within a few feet of the island's shoreline. Kenny cut the motor and Iz stood up on her seat, balanced a hand on the edge of the boat, and then jumped over into the water when we were just about to kiss the shore. She guided the bow up onto the sand. Kenny gave me a little shove.

"Man overboard," he said, climbing over the edge himself with the anchor in hand. He made sure one end of the rope was tied to the boat and then drove the anchor deep into the sand a few feet up the beach. Iz pulled the boat higher up onto the shore.

I looked around the island, thinking about what Iz had said, while the two of them beached the boat. It sounded as if everybody in Long Past Nowhere had decided to go ahead and let themselves believe that the bank money was buried here. I mean, a large sum of missing money? Deserted island? Nothing better to do with your time? Hello! I'd probably buy into the buried-treasure theory myself if I didn't happen to be related to the guy who had to go sleep with the fishes in order for the whole fairy tale to hang together.

I figured it was way more likely my father had just turned the boat loose as a false trail and then hauled off with the *mucho dinero* to someplace where they don't ask too many hard questions. And the truth was, I wasn't at all sure I liked that ending any better. I mean, the guy knew I was baking in Ma's oven and that my timer was set for just a few months away, and instead of sticking around to meet me someday, he chose to form a lasting relationship with a pile of cash? Oh, happy birthday to me!

I was smart enough not to point out any of my reasoning to Iz, given the mood she seemed to be in. It was clear she needed to believe the whole buried-treasure thing, the way some people need to believe in reality TV. If she wanted to buy into it so badly, no reason for me to be the buzzkill. Besides, I'd already figured out I could spend my time in Minnesota either (A) hanging with Kenny and Iz playing Pirates of the Corn and Soybeans, or (B) hanging with the Church

Ladies. Iz was a whole lot hotter than Mrs. Faltzkog, so I opted for A.

But something in me couldn't resist throwing out, "So how do you figure you'll be the one to finally crack the whole mystery of the missing money, Nancy Drew?"

Iz rolled her eyes and walked away.

As soon as her back was turned, Kenny leaned toward me and whispered loudly, "I know from past experience it ain't worth it, man; don't mess with Texas."

"I heard that!" said Iz. "Are you idiots coming with me or not?"

We wandered the island, beating our way around trees and through tall grass and underbrush. The island wasn't very big; we covered the whole thing from one end to the other in an easy hike. I guess it was pretty, or whatever nice thing you can find to say about a deserted hunk of land. But since there weren't any planks to walk or cannons to set off, or even any squawking parrots yelling "Arrrrggggg," it didn't seem as fun and piratey as I had hoped.

I pretended to memorize every crooked tree limb and the curve of every big rock as Iz pointed them out like some overly helpful Hollywood Celebrity Homes tour guide. She told me her family had spent a lot of time out there when she was a little kid, and I guess the place was a big deal to her, because she had made up silly names for almost everything: Acorn Academy for this one gigantic oak; Fairy Rock for a big boulder that sparkled in the sun; Fingers-to-Heaven for a jagged-topped ten-foot stump.

It all kind of blurred together for me. Since I was the one they were counting on to recognize a map of the island in my father's stuff, I figured we were out of luck unless I stumbled across something that was clearly labeled "Island" with an arrow pointing to a big red *X* and a scrawled *"buried treasure here."*

At least some good came out of the whole thing, though: our little wander through her happy childhood memories seemed to have cooled down Iz's bad mood by the time we were heading back home in the boat. So I thought it was safe to ask one of the questions that still dogged me. "Here's the other thing I was wondering: What are you going to do with the reward money when you collect the big bucks?"

I was wrong about the cooled-down part.

Iz turned on me, and her eyes could have melted the skin off my bones. "That part is my business," she snapped. "Not everyone is born a rich California smart aleck!"

I felt my jaw drop down and my inner demon rise up at the same time. "And not everyone's born a—"

"Time-out, you two!" Kenny suddenly bellowed from the back of the boat. "This is the part where Coach would make you both drop down and give him fifty."

Iz glared at me a minute. Then she stood up, whipped off her shorts and T-shirt to reveal a bikini underneath, and threw her watch down onto the seat. I admit it—my mouth dropped open and stayed open when she went for the T-shirt, so she got in the last word.

"You are just about the stupidest boy I've ever met!" Then she dived over the side of the boat and started swimming toward home.

Kenny shrugged at me and adjusted the boat's speed to putter. "Guess she's voted herself off the island."

We followed along, watching her slice through the water at top speed. My rage sizzled like sunburn under my skin, and then it drained down through my feet and out into the bottom of the boat. Finally I gave in and turned to Kenny.

"Uh—shouldn't we stop her or something? Looks like she's planning to Michael Phelps her way home."

He shrugged again. "She was the best swimmer on the tritown team before she quit this year; the distance back home is barely a warm-up to her. But we better follow close behind. If Mom catches one of us swimming without using the buddy system, we're grounded for a month. So watch to make sure Iz's head comes up for air once in a while."

I watched her windmilling arms for a few yards and then turned back to Kenny. "Seriously, what is wrong with her?"

Kenny shook his head. "She's a girl, dude. That's just how they are. I got two sisters and two girl cousins and a mom living in my house. There's no explaining them. You just stay out of their way when you can and keep your head down when you can't."

"Then why aren't you off tossing around the pig-skin with a bunch of your buddies instead of playing pirate?" I asked.

Kenny glanced over the side of the boat, either to

make sure Iz's head was still visible or to check if she was likely to hear us—I wasn't sure which.

"Look, man, Iz's family has had some really bad times lately," he said. "I mean, you might think you've got parent problems, but her mom and her dad, they both . . . although that don't make it right for her to trash-talk you like that. But this money—she really thinks it could fix things for her family. She's kind of . . . focused on it. And I don't mind trying to help her out." Then he grinned his usual grin—what I was starting to think of as the Kenny Grin. "Besides, Iz is the smartest kid in school. And I ain't exactly Einstein. I made her swear she'd do whatever it takes to get me passing grades next year so they don't bust me off the football team."

I thought about that a minute. "Okay, I won't ask you to fill in the blanks in the family soap opera. I guess it's not really my business. But I gotta tell you—Iz is right about my family having money. At least my stepfather seems to have a whole big bunch of it—and I'm not exactly living happily ever after."

Iz had reached shore. Kenny cut the motor back even more, and the two of us sat in the boat and watched her climb up the ladder, up the dock, up the sloping yard, and into Kenny's house. She never looked back.

Kenny waved his hand in the direction Iz had vanished. "I'm just saying, keep your head down and you'll be safer around her. It'll be all right; you'll see. She never stays ticked in the end."

Even as he said it, Iz was hurrying back down the dock toward us. She looked as if she'd worked off her anger; in fact, she looked a little freaked.

"What's the matter with you now?" Kenny asked.

She gave me a scared look and kind of hugged herself. "Trav, I think you better get over to your grandma's house. There's a sheriff's car sitting in her driveway, and my little sister says the deputy was over here asking where you were."

CHAPTER 8

For, like, a minute after Iz told me about the sheriff's car, I completely froze; all I could focus on was this series of film clips playing across the Trav's-Head Cinema—outtakes from every show I'd ever seen where the cop comes to the door to deliver the news that somebody's croaked. Who was dead? Gram? Ma? Then somehow, without really knowing how it happened, I was standing in Gram's kitchen looking at her and this big dude in a uniform sitting at the table with coffee mugs and cookies in front of them.

"Is something wrong with my mom?" I had to push the words out past an invisible hand that was around my throat, choking me.

"Your mother is fine," said Gram. Her face had its usual unreadable expression and she didn't look as if she'd been involved in a five-cow pileup or any other kind of emergency.

The guy got to his feet. "You're Travis?" he said, only it wasn't really a question. "I'm Deputy Anderson. Why don't you sit here so we can have a little talk."

He towered over me, making it clear I didn't have much of a choice. I sat on the edge of the chair across from Gram, and he sat down at the head of the table, where he could keep his eyes on both of us.

Gram spoke up. "Deputy Anderson and I have been discussing—"

But he interrupted her. "Thank you, ma'am—I can take it from here." I had been waiting to see if he was good cop or bad cop, but it seemed as if he had everything mixed up. Interrupting an old lady put you in the bad cop camp, right? But then sticking the "ma'am" in there kind of muddied the water.

Deputy Dude kept on talking. "I got a call after lunch from Mr. Svengrud down at the Big Store. Said you'd been in today spending a bit of money."

Far as I could tell, there weren't any hidden question marks anywhere, but it was clear he expected an answer from me.

"Uh—yeah?" I couldn't resist turning my answer

into a somewhat snotty question even though I was pretty sure that was a Taser on his belt. I mean, was it against the law to spend money around here?

Deputy Dude tossed me a look that convinced me to dial it down a notch. "Where else did you spend money in town today?"

"I bought some stuff for Gram at the grocery store, and I stopped for some burgers at the café and a soda at the gas station," I said.

He nodded after each place I mentioned, and I noticed he was making marks in a little notebook. What was going down here? Had the good people of Cowpoke decided to run the son of a bank robber out of town on some trumped-up shoplifting charge or something?

"Well, Travis . . ." Deputy Dude paused really long, like he was giving me time to confess to an ax murder before slapping the cuffs on me.

That barfy feeling from earlier was taking over my guts again; whatever was left of the pancakes, the burgers, and the caffeine was slamming around my insides, wrestling to see what would make it out first. I clamped my lips together, and I guess the deputy took

that as the prisoner's refusing to narc, because he settled his big, beefy forearms onto the table and leaned
in toward me to drop his atomic bomb.

"Looks like somebody was in town today spending money that came from that bank burglary a few
years back. The one that the FBI figures your father
was involved in."

There was dead quiet in the kitchen while I
watched the mushroom cloud explode across that
screen inside my skull.

Sometime after the explosion, I realized Deputy
Dude was still talking. "And I want to be real careful
here about not jumping to conclusions, but the fact is,
turns out you spent money every place the cash turned
up. So I need to ask you—"

Gram surged to her feet. For a minute I thought
she was going to latch on to Deputy Dude's ear and
yank him right on out of her kitchen, but instead she
nabbed the plate of cookies out of his reach and stood
glaring at him.

"Kyle Anderson!" she said, and you could hear a
rattlesnake shaking its tail behind each word. "If you're
insinuating—"

"Mrs. Stoiska—" He tried using his long-arm-of-the-law voice, but it was obvious that Gram was going to win this round.

She talked right over him. "Let me make one thing perfectly clear." She limp-marched over and put her hand on the doorknob. "Every penny that Travis spent in town today came out of my pocket. It was *my* money. If you're accusing *me* of something, I'll call my lawyer so we can talk about the matter further. But my grandson is off-limits. The boy hasn't done anything wrong. And I'd like you to leave my home."

Deputy Dude walked over to the door. It was clear from the way his face tightened up that he thought Gram's story was plenty fishy. But finally he lifted his hat for a moment, tilted his head toward Gram, and then settled the hat back down with a tap.

"Just doing my best to try to make things easier for you and the boy, Mrs. Stoiska," he said. "Because soon it could be out of my hands; how it all plays out from here will depend on the FBI. The two of you may be in for a few hard questions from them."

He looked over at me. "I understand that your grandma wants to protect you. But the fact is, there's been no sign of that money for fourteen years. Then you show up, and two days later some of the money turns up, too. If you know anything, it could save you a lot of trouble if you tell me before the big guns get here."

He turned and nodded one last time to Gram. "You know how to find me if either one of you has any more to say on the subject. And for now it would be best if your grandson stays a while longer rather than head right back to California. I think it's likely we're going to need to talk to both of you again soon."

Then he walked out of Gram's kitchen.

CHAPTER 9

As Deputy Dude walked out the door, the world switched over to slow motion. Gram lifted her hand and started walking back to me, but she seemed to be battling gravity with each move she made. She opened her mouth and sounds came out, but they were the grown-up speak of the old Charlie Brown cartoons, all "wah wah wah" noises instead of actual talking. I felt my face push against the thickened air to shake my head at her, and then I hauled my body out of my chair and back to my room, where I could close the door and be alone.

In the room where my father used to sleep.

After a while I guess my brain rebooted. Random thoughts started to drift around in my head, trying to form some kind of pattern. But it was like an all-black thousand-piece jigsaw puzzle: there were way too many pieces and none of them fit together just right. When I was a kid and I couldn't get puzzle pieces to fit, eventually I'd just pound one in where it didn't really belong. But no way I was jigsawing this mess together just by pounding at it.

I'd come to Minnesota looking for answers, and instead I just had piles of new questions. What I wanted more than anything was to talk it all through with somebody who knew me deep down. I took out my cell and stared at it. Ma? No way. She'd just refuse to talk about my father all over again.

I really wished it were as easy as texting Jason Kalooky. I could use a whole keyboard full of those little frowny faces to translate all the crappiness across the two thousand miles between us. But at the start of summer he'd shipped off to a wilderness survival camp to fight grizzlies or something—the kind of place where they outlaw cell phones. I had seen him only a couple of times since Christmas anyway, since Ma had hauled me kicking and screaming all the long way to my new stepdaddy's house. But even though we were in different towns and different schools now, Kalooky and I still texted all the time and also met up online to do some gaming.

Now that he was offline, I didn't really have anybody to talk to. It wasn't as if I'd been able to make a bunch of friends when I showed up at a new school midway through seventh grade. Everybody had already staked out his territory; being friendly to the new guy was too big a risk.

So with no one to call, I just lay there on an old Minnesota Vikings comforter, looking at the ceiling while Deputy Dude's words played tag inside my head. They always chased one another back to the point where he'd said I had to stick around so I could have another little chat with him or the FBI. I suddenly realized that the only thing worse than being trapped someplace you suddenly want to escape is knowing that even if you do get out, you have no place better to go.

That stupid walking catfish, man—does he even stop to think before he trots on out of his pond? What if he never finds water again?

At some point there was a knock, and I heard Gram's voice outside my door. "Travis, dinner's ready."

"I'm not hungry," I called back, which was a lie, of course, because even though my stomach still had some of that pro-wrestling action going on, I was pretty much always hungry. But I just couldn't talk to her right then; this dark suspicion, this thought about Gram, was squirming its way into my brain like one of those hungry parasitic worms, and I needed to face *it* before I faced *her*.

There was quiet on the other side of my door and then Gram spoke up again. "All right. I know how upsetting this must be for you. I'll let you have some time to yourself. I'll put your plate in the refrigerator in case you want it later."

And maybe her saying "later" was all it took, because my brain finally hit hibernation mode and I somehow fell asleep.

I woke up feeling like something inside my stomach was clawing for food. I picked up my cell to check the time: 3:23 a.m. I moved through the dark house as quietly as I could, got the plate of dinner out of the fridge, and nuked it in the microwave. Then I grabbed a fork and creaked open the back door, heading outside to the end of the dock to sit where I could swing my bare feet down over the edge. A busy breeze drifted its fingers under my nose; the lake smelled like secrets. Waves licked up against the rocky shore, and somewhere close by, a cricket violined his legs.

You almost could have thought it was an okay place to be.

I had just finished eating when the air shifted in that way that tells you somebody is hovering, even though you didn't really hear anything. I looked around and saw Iz standing behind me, outlined in stars.

"If you've come to push me in, you might as well get it over with," I said. "Feel free to hold my head under water too—you'd probably be doing me a favor."

"I couldn't sleep," she said. "And then I looked out and saw you down here. Can I sit?" She shifted from one foot to another.

I shrugged. "It's a free country."

She plopped herself down next to me, and I measured how much closer my toes were to the waves running up under the dock than hers were.

"Trav, that word you would have called me earlier if Kenny hadn't stopped you—I deserved that," she said. "I'm sorry I was such a you-know-what."

I shrugged again, but that invisible hand that had

been choking me since earlier in the day finally eased up a little and words jumped to my lips, ready to pour out. But I still wasn't completely ready to admit what I was afraid might be true about Gram, so I let something else jump out instead—something that surprised even me.

"Do you think my father might still be alive?"

"You think he's alive?" She said it real doubtful. Then her voice shifted and she went on. "Because his being alive would explain how some of the money is turning up now."

I nodded. Then I swung my head around and looked at her hard. "I'm trying to get used to the fact that everybody in this town is up in everybody else's business, but how exactly do you happen to know about the money turning up?" Then I added, "Not like you don't seem to know a little too much about everything."

"But you really think your father—" she started in again, but I cut her off.

"No. This time you're going to answer my question. Tell me what you know about what happened today with the money."

Iz leaned forward and peered down at her own

toes. "Well . . . you know how when you were in the grocery store, you knocked over all those beans? The checkout girl is Kenny's sister Kari. She said she didn't introduce herself because you were already so embarrassed, but at dinner tonight she told this whole story about how they found some of the robbery money in the cash drawer and they called the deputy and everybody remembered you shopping there because of the beans and that's why Deputy Anderson wanted to talk to you."

I could feel the gravity pushing down against my shoulders. I took a deep breath and noticed the strawberry smell of Iz's hair. But I didn't want to get distracted by Iz smelling good or gravity or anything else, so I forced my mind back to the point and said, "Okay, start over and fill in the blanks this time. Every last detail."

She started talking slowly, like you do when you know somebody doesn't understand a whole lot of English. "Kari works at the grocery store. She saw you in there today, and sometime not long after that, Mr. Svengrud from the Big Store came over and asked her boss if he could check her cash drawer. Mr. Svengrud, he's a bigwig around town—you know, always donating money to church and stuff—and he's friends with her boss. So they looked through the bills in her drawer, and of course Kari was watching because she was worried maybe she was in trouble or something. And then Mr. Svengrud pulled out this certain stack of twenties. Only they were all the old-fashioned kind of twenties, you know, that look different than the ones now?"

She paused and I nodded.

"And Kari couldn't figure out why Mr. Svengrud was so interested in them. She's like Kenny, kind of—she doesn't pick up on details."

Iz paused so long this time that I had to say, "And?"

"And finally Mr. Svengrud pointed out how even though they were the old style of money, they all looked brand-new. Really, really fresh. No way they'd been in and out of people's pockets for however long it's been since the government changed to the new twenties. And Kari would never have paid attention to them herself, but Mr. Svengrud, he notices stuff like that. Plus he's always been kind of obsessed with finding the robbery money. He's out digging on the island or trolling with this really expensive underwater camera all the time."

I could see now where this was headed. I interrupted her. "Probably what really happened is some geezer at the old folks' home finally broke open his piggy bank. But this Svengrud guy and the local RoboCops think they've stumbled over the bank-robbery money? That's stupid!" I said.

"No," said Iz, "that's not all. I had to Google it to understand, but there's this thing called 'bait money,' and that's what this turned out to be."

"You people are big on bait around here," I broke in.

Iz sighed real big and went on. "'Bait money' is money that banks keep alongside their other cash, only they write down the serial numbers of the bait money. Then, if a bank robbery happens and the bait money gets stolen along with the regular money, the police hand around lists of the serial numbers to the stores in the area. That way, if any of the money starts turning up, they can trace it to the spender."

I thought about that for a minute. "You're saying that Svengrud got this list, like, fourteen years ago and hung on to it for all that time? And he just happened to pull it out the day I turned up in town to spend some cash? Or maybe it was just a slower-than-normal day here in Manure-ville, so checking out serial numbers seemed like a fun thing to do."

"Well, he has been really interested in the robbery all along." She sounded a little defensive; maybe I needed to lay off the "manure" BS before she got ticked off again.

Iz kept on. "Some of the Big Store money was on the list, and he started checking with some of the other storeowners, to see if any of them had been paid in bait money too. Maybe he figured he'd be more likely to collect the bank's reward if he could turn over lots of information to the cops. And when some of the money in Kari's drawer matched the list, her boss asked her who'd been in shopping that morning, and she remembered you were there because of the beans. So when they called the deputy, they mentioned that maybe you had been the one who spent it . . ."

She stopped talking again, and I guess we were both focusing on what she'd said, piecing it all together. Then Iz kind of breathed out, real soft, "I guess everybody jumped to the conclusion that you had the money. But if you're sitting here trying to figure it out, then you must not have it. *Somebody* knows where it is, but it isn't you—right?"

I thought about how back in the olden days, before CNN, those big volcanoes used to take everybody by surprise, and when they'd dig up the village hundreds of years later, they'd find people trapped midmotion in lava. I think a big part of me had been statued in place since Deputy Anderson had left Gram's house. My head had been on this big emotional merry-go-round, but otherwise I'd been frozen in time.

But something in that moment on the dock changed everything. I was done being a Whac-A-Mole, handy to have around for whoever wanted to take a whomp at me. The next person to decide I looked like the town scapegoat had better find himself another goat. There had to be a bunch around here.

So I said, "Look, I'm only going to say this once. I don't have a single clue where the money is. And I really wouldn't care, except it's all anybody in this town ever seems to think about. And now, according to the deputy, I'm trapped here with all these people determined to frame me unless I can figure out who *does* have it." I could tell I was getting a little worked up but I kept going anyway. "So . . . you want to find the stupid money for some reason you won't tell me, and now I need to find it too, which I guess—whether you like it or not—makes us partners. We're like Bonnie and Clyde 2.0."

There was this long silence, and then Iz said, "Uh, Bonnie and Clyde were bank robbers. We're the ones trying to catch Bonnie and Clyde."

"Know-it-all," I muttered.

"Rich California smart aleck," she answered back. But she said it kind of sweetly this time, so I didn't mind. I mean, yeah, the girl was seriously annoying, and yeah, she was probably using me so she could collect the bank reward. But she was pretty hot, too. The hot thing seemed to be winning out over the other two, somehow.

I could feel her swinging her legs back and forth next to mine over the edge of the dock, but then she stopped. "So—don't get mad again—but do you really believe your father is still alive?"

I looked out at the dark lake stretching away from our feet. Had my father planted his bones in that big deep, or was he still walking around somewhere on solid ground?

The strange thing was, much as I couldn't wrap my head around what it would mean if dear Daddy-O was still around, instead of being dead the way I'd always been told, I had a whole different problem on my hands if it *wasn't* him spending the pirate loot. A problem that had been freaking me out even more than the possible reappearance of Ghost Dad. The problem I was finally making myself face.

I *had* spent lots of money in town that day. The bait money could have come from my hand. Because even though it was the one thing the town Gossip Girls apparently hadn't discovered yet—or at least, it hadn't spread as far as Iz—three people were in on the secret. I knew, and Gram knew, and she'd made sure Deputy Anderson knew too: The money I'd spent hadn't come with me from California. *My* money was still sitting in my bedroom. No, the money I'd spent in town had come from a person who had been in Cow Dung the whole time, before the robbery happened and ever since then, too. The money I'd spent had come from Gram.

So I wasn't thinking just about a daddy come back from the dead or how good it felt to talk to someone outside my own head or that word *partners*. Instead I was asking myself a question: If it was true that my father was Clyde, could it also possibly be true that my grandmother was Bonnie?

CHAPTER 10

What do you think?" asked Iz.

I jumped a little when she spoke, and for just a minute there I wondered if I'd gone so long without anyone to talk to that I'd actually asked Iz my question about Gram. But I could barely say it to myself; I knew there was no way I'd said it out loud.

I hit the rewind button to figure out what Iz's last question had been. I was used to doing that; my brain is always bouncing around to different things when I'm supposed to be paying attention. It drives my teachers crazy, so I'd learned how to backtrack to the last question mark for those times I need to pull something out of my butt and save myself.

"I don't want to talk about my father anymore," I said, thinking my way back to Iz's original question about whether my dad might still be alive. "And I don't want to talk about my grandma or Kenny or Kenny's sister or the deputy or Mr. Svengrud or the bait money." Iz opened her mouth to say something but I kept right on going. "I'll talk about them all again tomorrow. But right now, uh-uh."

It felt good—really good—talking to Iz about everything. But I wanted to think through this Gram thing some more before I called the FBI hot line, and if that meant our conversation was over for now, that was how it had to be.

Iz pulled her knees up and wrapped her arms around them. "Okay. What do you want to talk about, then?"

My mind went as blank as a flat screen when the cable goes out. It was like Ma always says: I didn't think things all the way through. It just hadn't occurred to me that Iz would stick around once I'd told her I didn't want to talk about the money anymore—I mean, that was why she was hanging out with me, right? No way I was going to be able to come up with something else interesting to say. With the whole school switchover, I had somehow become a complete dimwad at boy-meets-girl stuff. And Iz had made it clear there were land mines planted everywhere if I asked her the wrong question about herself. What did that leave us to talk about? Toxic chemical spills? The economic meltdown?

Finally, out of desperation, I said, "Uh . . . we could play 'I'd rather.'"

"'I'd rather' what?" she asked.

"Just 'I'd rather,'" I said. "It's this game we used to play at my old school. My language arts teacher, Mrs. Z., she had us play it every Monday. She'd ask an 'I'd rather' question, something that's personal but not personal-personal, and then everybody in class had to write an essay explaining why they chose the answer they did. And if she picked your answer as the best one, you won a prize. It was . . . fun," I said weakly.

Any minute I was sure the stars were going to jump out of their constellations and spell out the word *dweeb* across the sky. I mean, there I was, alone with this hot girl, and I decided the thing we should do was play language-arts games? That was, like, all-star dweeb, man. World-heavyweight dweeb. Take-your-mother-to-prom dweeb.

"Yeah, I guess it sounds . . . fun," said Iz. "But I don't think I get it."

I knew it was already going to take hours of painful surgery to get the "dork" tattoo removed from my rep. There was no point in trying to backpedal. So I said, "Okay, here. It's like if I say, 'Would you rather take a time machine into the future or into the past,' what would you answer?"

Iz lay her cheek down onto her pulled-up knees with her face turned toward me, and I could see her wrinkle up her nose while she thought about it. "You go first," she said. "What would you rather?"

"I'd rather go to the future every time, man. It can't get here soon enough for me."

"I think I'd rather go back to the past—it's like getting a do-over," said Iz slowly. She turned her face away and looked straight ahead. "Okay, do me another one."

"This one's easy," I said. "When I get stuck somewhere, I'd rather be . . ." I stretched out the "be" really long while I thought about my own answer. According to Deputy Dude, I was definitely stuck for the duration. So where would I rather be? Right that minute, sitting on the end of the dock in the deepest part of night, noticing the way that Iz's dark hair divided across her shoulders when she leaned forward to hug her knees, I couldn't think of anyplace.

"I'd rather be swimming," she said. "You know how when you've done a few laps you get in that zone —your mind just goes blank and the water lifts you up and you're strong but loose, all at the same time?" She was quiet a minute, and then she said, "Your turn."

"I'd rather be eating," I said.

She laughed and reached out to poke my side with her finger. "Be serious."

"Okay, here's the hardest one." The dorky game was going better than I had expected. "Would you rather be able to turn invisible or be able to grow wings and fly?"

"That *is* hard," she said, thinking a while and then turning to look at me again. "What did you choose?"

I grinned at her. "I cheated. I couldn't decide. But I won the prize that week anyway 'cause I wrote a killer essay for each answer. I mean, if I were invisible, I could sneak around and learn everything, right? Nobody could keep any more secrets from me. And flying —that's like swimming is for you, maybe? I'd just let go of everything that's dragging me down and spiral free, off into the sky."

"Free," Iz echoed. She stretched her neck back and stared up at the stars, so I did too. They seemed to have faded a little since we'd first started talking. Then she whispered something really low. I had to lean closer to her to try to hear.

"What?"

"Sometimes people fly away and never come back," she said again, still talking quietly.

I wasn't sure if that was an anti-flying vote or not, but something told me not to push her on the point. Besides, leaning in close that way, I could smell the strawberry again, and her ear curled like a seashell, and I wondered if her hair was really as soft as it looked when it brushed against her cheek as she turned her head to look at me again.

I leaned in a little closer.

Then suddenly this crazy laugh rang out, and Iz and I jumped apart as if we'd heard a gunshot. I looked around, convinced Kenny was going to pop out from behind a bush or something, and Iz rose to her feet.

"It's just a loon." She pointed out across the dark water. "They call out to one another like that. Bet you thought for a minute it was some psycho killer coming after us, right?"

She looked over at the eastern end of the lake. "The sky is starting to lighten. It must be close to morning, and Uncle Ken gets up way early. I better go." She hurried up the dock but turned to look back at me when she reached the yard. "I liked your game, Trav." Then she flicked her hand in a tiny wave and headed to Kenny's house.

The wind picked up and goose bumps rose along my arms. Flying versus invisibility—making a choice like that was nothing up against the no-win either-ors I had on my plate.

Would I rather find out my father was dead or alive? Somehow, knowing he could still be walking around somewhere didn't make me go all fluffy-bunnies with happiness like it probably should have. If he was just playing dead, didn't that mean he'd chosen to ignore me my whole life? And if so, was there anything I could do to make him come out of hiding? The only bait I had to offer him was my actual existence, and that hadn't been enough to interest him before now.

And if he really was dead, so it wasn't him spending the bank money, was it Gram? Just how many bank robbers was I going to find swinging from my family tree?

And would I rather be trapped here in Deputy Dude lockdown or heading back to the big house in California? I already knew life there was no walk on the beach. I'd been starting to think that maybe Minnesota wasn't so bad after all, even though there were more grain silos than stop signs in town. But now the friendly people of Podunk had apparently decided to string me up for something I didn't do.

If I could figure out who really was spending the money, the deputy would have to let me leave town if I wanted to, and I should be glad to get gone, right? I wasn't so sure. I still thought being here might help me figure out a bunch of stuff I needed to know. But I wanted staying or leaving to be *my* choice. I didn't know why it seemed different, but it did: getting to choose between two places where I didn't really fit somehow seemed better than just being trapped in one of them.

There was only one thing I knew for sure: I'd really, really rather go backwards in time and get one more chance with Iz before that stupid loon interrupted us than have to move forward and deal with all the crap a brand-new day was bound to bring me.

The loon suddenly cackled his crazy laugh again, and this creepy feeling spidered its way down the back of my neck. Even the local wildlife was messing with me. So I picked up my plate and headed inside to bed.

CHAPTER 11

I just couldn't seem to find the appropriate rule of etiquette that covered how to ask your grandma if she was a bigtime felon.

So by the time I wandered out of my bedroom at noon the next day, I knew what I had to do. I was going to have to sneak around behind Gram's back to figure out if she'd been sneaking around behind everybody else's. It seemed like the only choice I had if I wanted to be able to decipher the truth about my family. Not to mention if I decided I needed to get out of Dodge anytime before I was old enough to vote.

And I was going to need some help playing superspy.

I remembered Gram saying something to her posse about more fundraiser setup that afternoon, so the first step of the plan was to get myself out of help-ing with that. When I walked into the kitchen, Gram was washing dishes. By hand. Which maybe was some kind of clue all on its own. I mean, if you had bank-robbery bucks stashed away somewhere, wouldn't you head on down to the Big Store and have the King or-der you up the biggest darn dishwasher he could find?

I picked up the dishtowel and started drying. Gram gave me that look that adults get when they know you're up to no good; I guess taking on a chore without being asked at least three times first is like what they call a "tell" on TV poker.

But apparently Gram had as much on her mind as I did on mine, because after a moment she picked up the next plate and began washing it.

"Thanks for leaving me dinner last night. It was good," I opened.

"It's a pleasure to cook for someone besides my-self again." She handed me the wet plate. "Especially somebody who enjoys it the way you do. I'd forgotten how a thirteen-year-old boy can eat. That's one way you're exactly like your father. That and charming ev-ery Church Lady in sight."

"Uh, Gram . . . speaking of the Church Ladies—or really, I mean, about the church fundraiser . . ."

She stopped me. "Travis, I know that hearing the deputy's accusations yesterday upset you. And I understand better than anyone what it feels like when people around here suspect the worst of you. I know going to the fundraiser means you'll have to face a roomful of strangers—some of whom think you're up to no good. I'm sure that seems hard. But the best way to prove you didn't do anything wrong is to just march right into that church tonight with your head held high. If the people of this town can't deal with that, then they're the ones who should stay home."

It hadn't occurred to me that other people might already be suspicious of Gram—might think she knew something about the missing money. Stupid me. Just what kind of crap had she put up with over the years?

And what kind of rotten grandson was I for suspecting her myself?

"I don't mind going to the actual fundraiser," I said hurriedly, although the truth was, I wasn't sure which would be more painful: that, or the time my stepfather insisted on subjecting me to the birds-and-bees talk. "I was just wondering if I could maybe get out of helping with setup again today," I said.

"I hate to think of you spending so much time alone." Clearly she didn't really understand the social realities of my now loser life in California.

"Oh, I'll see if Kenny and Iz will take me out in the boat or something." It was strange, how guilty I was feeling; lying is one of my mad skills, and I lie to Ma all the time without thinking twice about it. Somehow with Gram it seemed different.

"I imagine they're more fun than a bunch of old ladies." Gram handed me the last plate and pulled another towel off the rack to dry her hands. "Travis, if Deputy Anderson happens to come by when I'm not here, you call me right away. I'll leave the church number on the counter. I'd rather you didn't talk to him alone. I don't want him fretting you again."

"I'll call you—trust me."

My plan was under way.

I knew Kenny and Iz were coming over—I mean, I had called them as soon as Gram pulled out of the driveway—but my insides still gave this little jump of surprise when there was a knock on the door. I pulled it open and my toes went numb when Iz walked in.

I guess my mind kind of drifted off too, distracted by the memory of that almost-kiss on the dock the night before, because next thing I knew, Kenny was giving me this big shove on the shoulder.

"Earth to Butter Head," he said. "What's with you today, bro? I've been talking to you for, like, five minutes."

Maybe I needed to learn to stay more alert when traveling in a foreign country. I could feel my face heating up, and Iz slid me a quick sideways glance.

"So I've got a plan," I said, before I could get distracted again. Or before I could change my mind, like I'd been doing over and over ever since Gram gave me her speech. But I didn't see any other options, so I made myself keep going. "And we've got to move fast. But before I tell you, you gotta promise that no matter what, we'll all decide together what to do about whatever we find. Even if it means you don't get to collect that reward money from the bank after all. 'Cause I'm, like, trusting you both here, bigtime."

"Yeah, yeah, Scouts' honor," said Kenny, except he made the hang-loose sign instead of whatever it is the Boy Scouts do with their fingers when they pledge. Which didn't make it exactly authentic, but I let it slide.

I looked at Iz, and after a long moment she put her closed fist onto her heart and nodded at me.

I didn't think I had to fill Kenny in on all the Deputy Dude details, since it was his sister who had fingered me as the town big spender. "Here's the deal," I said. "Since we know *I* don't have it, somebody else must be papering the town with the money. So one thing we're trying to figure out is if my father is alive out there somewhere, making like a big-bucks zombie."

"Say what?" said Kenny. "Do-over, dude! You mean your dad isn't dead? When did that happen?"

I wasn't sure if Kenny was behind on this part of the breaking news because Iz had kept our little late-night meet-up a secret from him or if he really did have trouble staying within the lines when he colored.

"He's *maybe* not dead. That's *one* thing we're trying to figure out."

"One thing?" said Iz. "What else is there—we

find your father, we find the money, right? Mystery solved."

"But he maybe *is* really dead," I said. "So we also have to figure out who else might have the money. I even wondered—just for a while—if maybe Gram had found the money somewhere and now she has it." I kind of mumbled that last part, pretending I was suddenly really interested in the beat-up kitchen floor. There was this big crack next to my foot. I wished it would open like one of those earthquake fault lines and swallow me right up.

"Your grandma?" asked Iz. She thought a moment. "Well, yeah, I guess she's an obvious possibility, but she's lived here the whole time. Why would she wait until now to start spending it?"

My breath heaved out in relief. Iz was smart. If she didn't think Gram was guilty . . .

"I don't *really* think Gram has it," I said. "It's just —maybe somehow she knows something without really knowing she knows it? Or maybe my father tried to contact her sometime—you know, sent her a post card or whatever—so she knows he's still alive? And anyway, it's like that game Clue—you know, where you eliminate the suspects and then whoever's the only one still standing at the end must be the killer. If we're going to do this right, we have to rule out Gram as a possibility." I could tell I was making about as much sense as my past year's geometry teacher.

"So about your dad," said Kenny. I guess he *was* having a little trouble keeping up. "Did he have, like, plastic surgery or something? If it was him, how come nobody in town recognized him while he was spending the money?"

Iz and I both whipped our heads around to stare at him.

Iz sighed. "I must be tired. I hate when Kenny thinks of something I didn't." She looked over at me. "Did you think of that?"

Kenny smirked while I shook my head.

"I guess if he is alive, he must be hiding out somewhere and maybe he has an accomplice. You know, somebody he's passing the loot along to," I said slowly. "Somebody who seems perfectly innocent so nobody suspects him. Or her."

"Like your grandma," Kenny said. Were we back to Gram being a suspect? I sent Kenny a shut-your-trap look.

"Or maybe . . ." started Iz. "You know, the newspaper said the FBI thought your dad had an accomplice for the robbery itself. Maybe that person's still around. Maybe when you turned up, they figured it was finally safe to start spending the cash because everyone would blame you for it."

I was opening my mouth to tell her what a genius idea this was when Kenny jumped in. "Like I said, maybe it's your grandma. Maybe she's the accomplice. Maybe she's really Grandma Stick-'Em-Up!"

"All right, enough grandma-ing!" I said. I wasn't sure why I was getting so ticked; after all, I'd been the one to bring up Gram in the first place. I'd spent half the night worrying about the same things Kenny was now saying. But it was like how you can trash-talk your best bud as much as you want, but as soon as somebody else starts in, you're all over him for it.

"There's this tiny outside chance that maybe Gram found the money somewhere *after* the robbery, but I won't believe she helped hold up a bank. She's *not* some granny-get-your-gun type!" I glared at Kenny. "Watch it."

"Boys, boys, peace out, already," said Iz. She turned

to me. "I thought you said we had to work fast on this master plan of yours."

"Yeah, okay," I said, giving Kenny one last don't-go-there look. "I think we have to search Gram's house. To see if there are any clues that my father might really be alive. Like an address or a phone number or a post card he sent from Rio or something." For just a second I flashed back to that talk in Gram's truck, where she'd told me about when my father had vanished. Had she said she'd never heard from him again? Or had never *seen* him again? I couldn't remember exactly. And anyway, would it really be such a big deal if Gram had lied to me?

Iz nodded. "I'm still hoping there could be something like a treasure map."

"Or just a big pile of bank cash," said Kenny.

Iz looked at him really hard. "We have to use our brains while we search 'cause the clues might not be obvious. And we better make sure to put everything back like we found it." She turned to me. "We don't want your grandma to suspect we searched her house. When's she coming home, anyway?"

"I'm supposed to meet her at the church at five o'clock," I said.

Iz checked her watch and then walked into the living room and looked from one end of Gram's small house to the other. "We only have a couple hours. I'll do her bedroom and the bathroom. There's probably girlie stuff in those places."

I nodded.

"Kenny, you start with the kitchen," she went on. "You spend all your time eating—that should be an easy room for you. Just call us if you find anything that doesn't belong. And look everywhere!" She turned to me. "What about you?"

"I'm going to start with Gram's desk," I said. "It's got all those little cubbies and drawers and stuff."

There was silence as we each started off on our own personal spy missions. But after just a few minutes, Kenny spoke up from the kitchen. "Bro, can I take a food break? I'm getting hungry."

"Yeah. If you can find anything I've missed, you're welcome to it," I said.

"Kenny? Pay attention to what you're doing instead of to your stomach," Iz called out from Gram's bedroom.

"No wonder I always wanted to be the robber when we used to play cops and robbers. This searching-the-house thing is boring when you can't rip apart pillows and stuff like they do on TV," said Kenny. "At least let's crank some tunes."

"I don't have my iPod speakers here," I said. "But you can try Gram's radio."

"You'll be sorry," Iz yelled out. I suddenly had a horrifying thought: What if Kenny was into country music? We were sitting smack in the middle of cow county, after all. My nerves were strung out enough without somebody strumming across them like a banjo.

Fifteen minutes later Judas Priest was telling me "You've Got Another Thing Comin'" on some heavy-metal station Kenny had somehow scrounged up, and I had realized the kid was dead right about both the hungry and the boring parts of playing cop. Then Iz came out of the bedroom carrying a box. She set it down next to me and walked over to click off the radio. "How can you listen to that stuff?"

Kenny walked in from the kitchen.

"Where you'd find that?" I asked, zeroing in on the giant slab of pie he was eating out of his hand. "That wasn't here at lunchtime."

"Freezer," said Kenny, showing off a huge bite of

apple while he talked. "I searched the whole freezer real carefully just like you said, Iz." He waved his half-eaten wedge toward the kitchen. "S'more where this came from," he added to me.

"A little focus here, please?" said Iz, grabbing my arm as I turned toward the kitchen. "What happened to 'we've got to move fast'? You can both think about your stomachs later." She waved toward the box. "I found something a lot more important than pie. There're newspaper articles and stuff about the bank robbery at the top of this. Maybe there's other stuff about your father underneath."

The pie suddenly didn't look so good; I guess the truth was, I was counting on our *not* finding anything in Gram's house to incriminate her.

"Finding the articles doesn't mean anything," said Iz. Maybe she'd noticed my turning green or something. "Your grandma was his mom—she'd keep those just because . . . you know?"

"My mom buys ten copies every time I make the sports section and sends them to all our relatives," said Kenny. "Moms like to show off like that."

Iz heaved this big sigh. It seemed as if she had to throw one of those at Kenny or me every hour just to keep herself from filling up with hot air and floating away. "Not helpful, Kenny."

"Where'd you find the box?" I asked while Kenny made a what'd-I-do expression with his hands and face. I squatted down and set the cover of the box aside.

"It was under her bed. There's nothing else interesting in her bedroom."

I started pulling stuff out, making little piles. The smell of old school-library books rose up from the box. There were yellowed newspaper clippings and a beat-up photo album and yearbooks and a bunch of random pieces of paper. I picked up the top newspaper article and stared at a photo of a guy in an army uniform. He looked a lot like me. My father.

I realized Kenny had said something, so I made myself look up and say, "Huh?"

"I'm done in the kitchen. You want me to take over the desk so you can start in on this stuff?" he asked.

The piles of papers were pulling me in like an alien magnetic beam. Another part of me felt like you do when it's report-card day and you haven't slit open the envelope yet; whatever's inside could be waiting to bite you in the butt. I took another look at the piles of junk and then I checked out the box's cover.

"Doesn't look like there's any money here," I said. "And this is covered with six years of dust. I'm guessing it's been a long time since Gram crawled around on the floor to stick things under her bed, so she won't miss it. I'll hide it in my room before I leave and look at it tonight. That way we can keep working on the rest of the rooms while she's still gone. I'll keep going on the desk."

"I'll move on to the bathroom," said Iz. "Kenny, why don't you look in the coat closet and in that cedar chest there."

I had just gone back to flipping through phone bills and church bulletins when I thought I heard gravel crunching outside. Had Deputy Dude come back to try some water torture on me? I got up and went to look out the kitchen window.

Gram was getting out of her truck.

CHAPTER 12

My heart slammed against my ribs like a pinball bouncing off the flipper. I ran into the living room.

"Gram's home!" I worked to dial down my volume. "We've got about ten seconds to get this stuff put away."

Iz stuck her head out of the bathroom, gave me a panicked look, and then went back in, slamming the door behind her. Kenny started throwing blankets back into the cedar chest. I scrabbled around on the floor, stuffing newspapers and other junk back into the box. The lid wouldn't fit, so I grabbed it and the box and ran toward my room just as I heard the back door opening. I whipped the box under my bed and then took two deep breaths, trying to put on my Mr. Cool mask before heading back out to face Gram.

"Kenny," I heard Gram say from the living room,

"what are you children doing in the house? Why on earth aren't you outside on such a beautiful day?"

"Well, I got to confess, Mrs. Stoiska." I froze on the other side of my bedroom door. Was that all it took? She hadn't even gotten out the thumbscrews, and Kenny was already acting like a narc?

"We got real hungry, so we came in and ended up eating most of your pie from the freezer. I'm sorry if you were saving it for something special." You gotta hand it to him—turned out he could lay it on as thick as a Minnesota accent when he needed to. I came out of the bedroom.

"Sorry, Gram," I said, hoping the pie theft would account for the redness I could feel on my cheeks. "We were starving."

Gram gave me this long look, making it pretty clear that she still had that mom skill. The one where she could sniff out a lie in two seconds flat. And between snooping through her house and turning her into a bank-robbery suspect, I guess it was no surprise I was sending out guilt waves.

Finally she turned and walked into the kitchen. I looked at Kenny and we followed her. She peered at the one little slice Kenny had left in the pie dish. "I didn't even remember it was there," she said. "You boys were welcome to it, as long as it hadn't gone bad."

"Best pie I've had in ages, Mrs. Stoiska," Kenny said. "Better than Grandma Gudrun's, even. Maybe if you don't mind, I'll just finish off this last little bit so that you can wash the pan."

I glared at him while he scarfed up the rest of the pie without leaving me even one little bite, but Gram's face relaxed at the compliment to her cooking. Then she looked around. "Isabella isn't with you?"

"Uh, she's in the bathroom," I said, waving vaguely in that direction.

"You know girls—takes them forever," said Kenny. "I pretty much never get a chance in there now that we've got even more of 'em living at my house."

Iz walked into the kitchen. "Oh, like you don't spend an hour in front of the mirror every morning searching for whiskers. Hello, Mrs. Stoiska." A dust bunny big enough to be a dust elephant was hanging off the back of Iz's shorts, but I figured it was probably better if I didn't reach over to brush it off.

"Hello, dear," said Gram. "Kenny's mother asked me to send the two of you home to get ready for the church fundraiser. We'll see you there later on. I forgot the hotdish, so I had to come home too." She looked me up and down, and her eyes stayed stuck on my shirt. I looked down and realized it was covered with dust from the box. When I lifted my head again, that x-ray look was back.

"You might want to put on a clean shirt, Travis." Gram's voice sounded cold. She finally broke eye contact, picked up the pie dish, and headed for the sink. I'd been spying on her. Now she didn't trust me. We were just one big happy family.

Iz gave me the thumbs-up sign and left.

"Later, dude," said Kenny.

I was now on bad terms with Gram and most of the rest of the town, but at least I'd have two allies tonight.

I couldn't help thinking about that box under my bed while I changed my shirt. But there was no time to look through it right then; Gram was already convinced I had been up to no good, and hiding out in my room would only make her more suspicious. Fortunately, when I came out, she seemed like back-to-normal Gram—not saying a whole lot, but not giving me that x-ray look, either.

I hated to rock the boat, but finding the box had made me want to start fishing even harder for information about my dad. So when Gram handed me the dish holding the food for the fundraiser and reached out for her car keys, I nodded toward that lumpy fish key rack.

"So, Gram? I know about the bank-robber thing and the rough edges, but there has to be some good stuff about my father too, right?"

Gram froze. Then she took the dish from me, set it onto the counter, and put her hands onto my shoulders, just for a second, before her hands dropped. "There was so much 'good stuff,' Travis. I know that everybody—even me, I'm realizing—has been focusing on the mistakes he made. But your father had some marvelous qualities too."

She leaned against the counter. "He loved his people the same way he did everything else: full tilt. It was hard sometimes to be on the other side of that love, because he didn't think through how concerned we would be when he took all his risks. But he was always genuinely repentant afterward. And he stuck by his loved ones no matter what."

"But he and Ma ended up . . . not together. Even though she was pregnant."

There was a long pause. "I do believe he cared about your mother, Travis, but their relationship was new, and as you just pointed out, it got complicated very quickly. And John was struggling at that point. It's something you should probably talk about with your mother. There are some things that only the two participants can truly understand about a . . . romantic relationship."

I suddenly felt a strong need to make sure there wasn't a single wrinkle on my T-shirt. Out of the corner of my eye, I saw Gram smoothing the corners of the aluminum foil covering the fundraiser food, making sure it was really tight. Really, really tight.

Finally Gram pushed off from the counter and straightened her shoulders. "I'm thinking about the loyalty he showed Carl. I told you that Carl stepped in as a father figure when your grandfather died. As John got older, Carl changed; he'd make plans with John and then not show up. But even in high school, John still made a point of stopping by Carl's house every couple of weeks. He brought him groceries and cleaned up the place. Carl's always been too proud to accept much help from most people, even as sick as he is now, but somehow he was willing to accept help from John. One of the things John was taking so hard that last summer was that Carl was finally losing his house, and John wasn't sure how to help him."

Gram glanced at the clock and grabbed up her keys. "Goodness, you're turning me into a regular chatterbox, Travis. We're late!"

Gram talked only once on the way into town, and that was to mutter, "They better have left us something other than that Jell-O concoction of Mimi Ingersoll's to eat. Mayonnaise and Jell-O! I'd rather be tarred and feathered."

Mayonnaise and Jell-O? I felt my gut tighten up. But I wasn't sure if it was the thought of a food combination even Kenny would likely avoid or Gram's mention of tarring and feathering. From what I remembered of middle-of-the-night Westerns on cable, that was what good old-fashioned townsfolk did when they wanted to hand out some vigilante justice.

And guess who was likely to be first in line the next time the local farmers cleaned the feathers out of their chicken coops?

CHAPTER 13

When we got to the fundraiser, first thing I saw, swear on a Bible (after all, it *was* a church), was a cage full of chickens sitting in the parking lot. The tar was not yet visible, but there were plenty of village elders to do the deed. The deputy and a bunch of other old dudes were milling around. I thought I recognized one of them as Apron Guy from the grocery store, even though he wasn't wearing his work getup. The whole group of them turned and laid their eyes on me as I climbed out of the truck.

Gram raised her chin up into the air in their direction. "Good evening, boys. Travis, get the hotdish." She marched toward the church. Deputy Dude scrambled to hold open the door for her. I trotted up right behind her with the big glass dish balanced in both hands so he had to hold the door for me, too.

"Nice night for a fundraiser, Deputy," I said, giving him my best it-wasn't-me-who-shot-the-spitball look.

Dude just gave me Taser-eyes for an answer.

Before he could whip out the handcuffs or the bucket of tar, I scrammed down to the room where I'd helped set up tables the day before. It looked as if the entire population of Chicken Scratch had gathered there, and they all stopped whatever they were doing to check me out, as if they'd just seen my face plastered on a "Wanted: Dead or Alive" sign. I had just about decided there was no way I was waiting around for them to Judge Judy me when Kenny and Iz walked over. Iz took the glass dish out of my hands and Kenny fist-bumped me.

Okay, so the *entire* town didn't hate me.

"Bro, you brought Tater Tot hotdish," Kenny said, pulling the aluminum foil off the top of Gram's dish as Iz set it on a table loaded with other food. "Touché!"

Huh? I looked at Iz.

"Kenny likes to pick out a new word of the day once in a while. He doesn't really care if he actually uses it right," she said.

I shifted my eyes toward the torch-bearing villagers. "I'm not feeling it. Maybe I'll just take off."

"Ah, ignore 'em, man," said Kenny. "They're just hungry. They'll forget all about you once they start eating. Besides, we got six kinds of Jell-O. Stay away from Mrs. Ingersoll's, though—she puts carrot scrapings in hers. But Mrs. Tunsen, she goes all out with these little multicolored marshmallows and Cool Whip."

Before I could suggest he get his own gig on the Food Network, this football-jersey-wearing mammoth swaggered over to us. "Nelson," he said, nodding to Kenny, real man-to-man for two guys who were barely old enough to shave.

Then he turned to Iz. "So nice they let you out once in a while, Izzzz-abella." He smirked while he said it, but I thought that just proved the local connection between football and lowered IQ levels; man, I'd been in town only a few days and I knew better than to mess with her. I could tell by the look on her face that if this bruiser wasn't careful, Iz was going to blast him back to the Ice Age.

Finally he turned to me. "Who's your new little friend, Izzzz-abella?" Dude was oozing attitude and testosterone in equal parts. Considering we were in a church, I probably should have given him the benefit of the doubt and figured there was some really sad story explaining why he was acting like a Neanderthal. I guess I'm not that good a person. I was fine with hating him on sight.

Without waiting for an answer, the brute looked back at Kenny and said, "Football players are sitting over in the corner, Nelson," and swaggered off again. "Svengrud" was spelled out in big letters across his shoulders.

Kenny glanced in the direction Mr. Congeniality had headed, then gave Iz a sad puppy-dog look.

"Oh, go on and sit with the ster-idiots. I don't care." Iz glared and crossed her arms across her chest.

Kenny gave me a sheepish look. "If you wanna come too . . ."

For some reason, the story about the rugby team who crashed in the mountains and then eventually started eating one another to survive came to mind. All things considered, I figured I was better off not finding out what Svengrud and his buddies might be cooking up for me.

"Bro, I'd rather eat than be eaten, but thanks anyway." I waited until he'd headed off before turning back to Iz. "Svengrud?" I asked. "Heir to the Big Store Kingdom?"

"Daddy's own little darling. Gets anything and everything he wants handed to him like he's a prince or something."

This party was just getting better and better. I wanted to ask Iz why the prince wasn't acting so charming, but then this woman stood up in the center of the room and raised her arms for quiet.

"Everyone, I'm Pastor Jackie. Thank you all for coming. I especially want to welcome our visitors tonight! I know you can't wait to get to all this wonderful food the Church Ladies have prepared. The donation baskets are here at the end; we appreciate whatever you can contribute. And don't forget the special event up in the parking lot afterward—remember to buy your tickets from the men's group!"

She waved her hand toward a row of tables over on the side wall where some of the men from outside were now standing. I wondered if they were selling tickets for my tar-and-feathering; it seemed like one way to make sure their fundraiser was a whomping success.

The pastor continued. "The Sunday-school

children are going to sing us a little song before grace. Children?"

A bunch of munchkins gathered around her and belted out "Jesus Loves Me." One little girl in front seemed to think she was Hannah Montana, swinging her hair and pretending her fist was a microphone while her mother snapped photos.

After the applause died down, the pastor said, "Now, let's please bow our heads."

Since all the people in the room had their eyes closed, I thought it was the perfect time for me to send up a little prayer of my own, asking the Big Guy Upstairs to levitate me out of there or maybe turn me invisible while nobody was looking. But I guess His ears were still ringing from the munchkin singing, because I hadn't gotten my answer by the time we reached "Amen."

Then Iz and I were elbowed aside by a stampeding herd of small fry on their way to the food tables. Note to self: *don't ever let yourself get trapped between the livestock and the feeding trough.*

Two little girls came over and grabbed hold of Iz's hands. "Aunt Jen says you both should come sit with us," said the smaller one. She hid under Iz's arm and peeked up at me with eyes as big and gray as Iz's.

The bigger munchkin giggled. "You're the bank-robber boy! We talk about you all the time at my house. Do you really have all the money hidden somewhere?"

I shot Iz a look and she shrugged. "That's Kenny's little sister, Krissy. And the shy one here is my sister, Linnea."

Krissy worked on dislocating Iz's arm, yanking her toward the food. "Come on, I'm hungry."

It didn't seem like Jesus was going to beam me up anytime soon, so I figured I might as well eat while I was waiting for My Man to do that saving thing he's gotten all the press for.

We worked our way down the food tables. It was a whole new universe of chow choices from what I was used to in California; nothing even pretended to be healthy. There wasn't a hunk of tofu in sight, although I guess Mrs. Tunsen could have hidden some under the Cool Whip. I loaded up and headed for the table where an adult-size version of Krissy was sitting next to Gram.

"You must be Trav. I'm Kenny's mom, Jen. Thank you for finding my butter head!" She got up and gave me a big hug that started all the Jell-O wobbling on my plate. She turned back to Gram. "Lois, these dark eyes. He looks just like—"

"Let the boy sit, Jen." A big blond guy next to her stood up and pulled a chair out for Iz. "He's probably starving." Then, as soon as I set my plate down, he stuck a hand out and said, "Ken Nelson, Sr. We've heard a lot about you from our boy and Iz."

We shook hands the old-school way, and then he gave me back my arm so I could start in on the taste-testing. I pretty much checked out of the conversation for a while, focusing on working my way through a rainbow of Jell-O. I had just found what had to be Mrs. Ingersoll's when Big Ken spoke up.

"Almost time for them to wrap up at the ticket table. Anybody here still need to buy some?"

"We've already got ours." Iz and the little girls each held up a colored slip of paper.

"I'm gonna win, Daddy!" Krissy flapped hers overhead.

Gram started fishing around in her purse. "Travis, go over and get yourself some tickets so you can play too. Here." She handed me a twenty.

I almost crossed my fingers like you do to ward away vampires. Wasn't I already in enough trouble from spreading around Gram's stash of dead presidents? But my breath whooshed out when I looked at the bill more closely. It was a normal one, with the colors and all; no way it could be fourteen-year-old bait money.

"Thanks, Gram," I mumbled.

Krissy grabbed one of my arms. "Can we help you pick? Pretty please with cherries on top?"

I sent Iz a what-do-I-do-now look and she got up, taking Linnea's hand. "We'll all help."

We headed for the row of tables where the old dudes were hanging out. Each table held different-colored slips of paper with numbers on them. It looked as if a bunch of them had already been taken. King Svengrud was standing behind one of the tables; I handed over the twenty, feeling like I was signing my own execution notice.

He immediately gave the bill the once-over. That saying "if looks could kill"? I'm guessing someone invented that one for the expression on old Svengrud's face when he realized I was in the clear this time.

"All right, pick yourself four tickets," he snapped.

I didn't have a clue as to what game we were playing, so I shrugged. "Whatever."

"No, no, you got to think lucky. What's your favorite color?" asked Krissy.

I couldn't resist yanking her chain. "Uh . . . black?"

"No, silly, one of these colors." She pointed at the tables.

"I'm not exactly Mr. Lucky these days," I said. "You pick a color for me."

She clapped. "Pink! Now, what day is your birthday?"

"November forty-first."

Her forehead wrinkled up while she thought about that.

Iz pinched me on the arm. "He's just teasing you, Krissy. Come on, what's your real birthday?"

"November fourteenth," I admitted.

Krissy scanned the pink tickets but then stuck out her lower lip. "Somebody already took pink fourteen. But here's yellow fourteen."

"Okay." I took the ticket from her. "You each go ahead and pick me one more and we'll be done—it doesn't really matter to me."

You would have thought they were choosing between five hundred flavors of ice cream. I was watching Iz trying to decide between blue eleven and green fourteen when I felt someone tug on my sleeve. I looked down.

"I got you purple fourteen," said Linnea in this really soft little voice. She handed me a purple ticket. "I like purple the best. My ticket is purple number seven."

"Uh . . . great," I said. I was as mystified about how to talk to girls in the munchkin size bracket as I was about how to talk to ones my own age. But she seemed to be waiting for something else, so I added, "I bet you'll beat me."

She got this big, goofy grin on her face, and I could see where a bunch of her teeth had fallen out.

"I like you even if you are a bad boy," she said, ducking her head down and taking hold of my hand.

Iz and Krissy walked over just then to hand me the tickets they'd picked out for me, and we let ourselves be jostled out of the way by other ticket pickers.

"Now what?" I asked.

"Five minutes, folks," boomed out the Big Store King. "Just five more minutes to buy yourself a winner! The fun starts outside in ten!"

"Almost time for the chicken game!" squealed Krissy. "Let's go."

The whole basement full of people started pushing and shoving their way upstairs as if we were on the *Titanic* after it had had that fender-bender. I would have held back but Linnea yanked me onward.

"You have to come see if you win." I let her pull me along.

Once we made it outside, we followed the crowd to the back corner of the parking lot. Everybody was gathering around this big square area marked off on the pavement with red paint.

Deputy Dude was directing traffic. "Pick a side, folks. Just stand back of the paint lines. We want everybody to get a view of the fun."

Linnea hauled me through the horde of bodies up to the front of the crowd. Somehow we got separated from Iz and Krissy, but Linnea squeezed the two of us into a spot along the paint marks. In front of us, inside the square, was a small area with a little fence around it. Inside the fence, lying on the pavement, was a big piece of plywood with a bunch of numbered squares. Next to the fenced-in area was the cage full of chickens.

"Just what exactly is this game?" I asked Linnea, nervous about being trapped up front where they could easily grab me when the tar was hot enough. But Deputy Dude held up his arms for quiet before she could answer.

"Folks," he said. "First round's the blue tickets. Tell the good folks about our blue ticket prize, Delbert, and then grab yourself a bird."

Apron Guy from the grocery store stepped up. "First round is the ice cream prize, everybody. You win this round and you win yourself a quart of ice cream every week for the next year."

The crowd clapped real loud while Apron Guy went over and grabbed himself a chicken. The bird squawked and fanned its wings, and somebody yelled out, "Don't let it drop the big one before the big game, Del," and everybody laughed.

Apron Guy carried the chicken over to the fenced-in area and set it down inside. The bird kind of pranced around, pecking at some seeds or something on the plywood, while the crowd went nuts. People were yelling out numbers and waving blue tickets in the air. Every so often the bird stopped and posed its head like a chicken supermodel. When that happened, everybody shut up.

Suddenly the bird dropped an A-bomb on number

seventeen. The crowd let out this big disappointed sigh, except for one lady who started leaping up and down and squealing, "Seventeen! He hit seventeen! That's me! I'm the winner!"

"Tiffany Tinboldt's got herself some ice cream, folks. Let's all give Tiffany a round of applause."

Tiffany ran around and around the inside of the square, raising her fists up over her head like Rocky and whooping while everybody else cheered.

Holy crap, dodo — I don't think we're in California anymore.

I gaped over at Linnea. "That's it? That's the whole game? A chicken takes a poop and somebody wins some ice cream?"

Linnea giggled. She'd certainly gotten over her shyness around me. "We're supposed to call it chicken-drop bingo, but Kenny calls it chicken-poop bingo. Once he even said chicken-sh—you know, that word we're not supposed to say."

The chicken was back in the cage with its buddies while a guy mopped up the plywood. The Hannah Montana–wannabe and some of her friends jumped around in the middle of the square waving pompoms in the air while the rest of us waited for round two.

Then Deputy Dude shooed us all back behind the paint marks again. "Time to get out your pink tickets, folks. Velma, come on up here and tell everyone about the pink ticket prize."

Velma told us all about the big bowling bonanza at the Bowl-O-Rama. Then she grabbed herself a clucker and set it loose on the plywood. Turned out pink wasn't so lucky for Krissy after all; that chicken crapped almost instantly for some guy in a baseball cap who looked as if he'd already swallowed a bowling ball. We worked our way through most of the crayon box and most of the chickens without anybody I knew getting crapped on, but then Deputy Dude waved for quiet again.

"Purple tickets, folks. Last round of the night is the purple round. One more big prize left to go." Linnea squeezed my hand. I looked down and saw her clutching her ticket for purple seven in her other hand.

"Milo, come on over here and give us the rundown on the purple prize."

King Svengrud trotted front and center. "Our last lucky winner gets to come on down to the Big Store and pick themselves out a new bicycle. We've got all the latest models on hand." I heard Linnea give this excited gasp, and her grip on me tightened even more. It was like holding hands with a python.

The King latched on to a chicken and plunked it down onto the plywood. This last clucker was a real ham. It milked its moment of glory like it was Miss Piggy in front of the paparazzi. Every time it paused and cocked its head, there'd be this big intake of breath from the crowd, as if everybody figured there was no way the bird could hold it in any longer. But then it would get back to prancing around. Finally, just when I thought maybe it was going to keep its little chicken legs crossed forever, I swear the thing looked straight at me with its beady eyes and then laid down a giant green glob on number fourteen.

"Fourteen," called out King Svengrud. "Step on up, lucky number purple fourteen."

People were turning their heads to look one way and then the other, trying to see who was going to step forward and claim the Big Store bike. Meanwhile, I was rethinking that whole invisibility versus flying thing. It had just never occurred to me to plan ahead for the day when a chicken would poop on my bingo square. And I was definitely feeling too chicken to go ahead and claim my prize. The whole town already thought I had spoiled their years of digging fun by coming up with the pirate loot and spending it myself. Now I was going to waltz right up and ace them out of their chicken-crap prize? Right. Invisibility would have been really useful in that moment.

But since I couldn't become invisible and Jesus still hadn't levitated me, I just turned my head from side to side like everybody else and pretended I didn't have a clue who the winner was. Except I had forgotten about Python Girl.

Linnea suddenly dropped my hand. She was turning around and raising her finger to point at me, her mouth a big round *O*, when I figured out what she was up to. I grabbed her finger midair and leaned over close to her ear.

"You're the real winner. You picked purple fourteen for me. You take this ticket up there and tell them you won that new bike." I stuck purple fourteen into her hand, spun her back around, and gave her a big shove forward into the center of the square.

"Linnea?" called out Deputy Dude. "Do you have the winning ticket? Step on up, little lady— don't be shy."

Linnea nodded and held up the ticket for purple fourteen high over her head.

And then she opened her mouth and said, as loud and clear as a foghorn, "Here it is. Purple fourteen. Bank-Robber Boy gave it to me."

Even the chickens stopped clucking while everyone turned to stare.

Until somewhere in the back of the crowd, on the other side of the square, a man's voice called out, "That's my kid. My kid's the winner! Hold up there, kiddo—here comes Daddy!"

CHAPTER 14

For just a second I think I really believed that the crowd was going to part and my father was going to come rushing out to help me claim my prize. That some guy dressed in a military uniform like the one I'd seen in the newspaper—somebody with the same eyes as mine—was going to come over to me and—

I didn't know what I thought. What exactly would back-from-the-dead Daddy do the first time he met me? I didn't have a clue.

I stood there frozen in place, watching as people got knocked to one side or another because the Daddy Voice was barreling his way forward through the crowd, still yelling out things like, "Hold on, kiddo, I'm coming."

Except, when the Daddy Voice finally reached the

front, I could tell right away that it wasn't *my* family reunion that was busting up the bingo fun. The party pooper in this case was a drunk guy who didn't match up with my pappy's photo in any way. I heaved in a big breath.

The Daddy Voice staggered into the row of chicken-poop cheerleaders, knocking Hannah Montana sideways so she tripped over the girl beside her, and next thing we knew, there was this tangle of little girls and pompoms thrashing around on the ground, and mothers were running forward and people were hollering and everybody was generally getting in the way of Deputy Dude, who was clearly trying to catch up to the Daddy Voice before he caused any more multi-tween accidents.

Even though it was clear he wasn't my daddy dearest, the Daddy Voice was still headed straight for me. Or as straight as somebody in his condition could head. And he didn't look like he was planning to give me a welcome-to-the-village hug when he reached me. Maybe this guy was one of Crazy Carl's friends? The town loons generally seemed to have it in for me around here.

I suddenly took in the fact that Linnea was as

frozen in place as I was, and she was standing directly in front of me. A few more seconds and the Daddy Voice was going to roll right over her on his way to me.

I leaped forward. Somehow I scooped up Linnea and hauled us out of there. I didn't stop until we were back behind the church building with nobody else in sight.

I set Linnea down and leaned over at the waist, letting my head hang and resting my palms on my knees while I sucked in air. Python Girl wasn't as light as she looked.

Linnea made this little hiccupping sound, and I turned my head to check her out. Snot streamed down her chin as big round tears rolled out of her eyes.

"Is Daddy gone?" she said.

"Daddy?" I repeated. "You mean—you mean that guy back there was your dad?"

Linnea nodded and wiped her nose on her bare arm.

Great. I'd just rescued the kid from a reunion with her own father.

But that waste case was Linnea's dad? And Iz's dad too?

And I thought I had father problems.

I really had no clue what to do next. I wanted to just start walking until I fell off the world, like those explorers used to think would happen if they sailed too close to the edge of the map. But I knew I couldn't leave Linnea there all alone and dripping snot.

Fortunately, just then Kenny loped around the church and pulled to a stop in front of us. He didn't look like his usual jolly self. Linnea flung her arms around him and wiped her face on his shirt.

"Bro, touché," he said to me.

"You know, dude, I'm not sure you really understand what that word means."

He shrugged and kind of hoisted Linnea up. She swung around to hang on his back like a spider monkey and buried her face in his neck. "Whatever. Gotta get Squid here back to my folks. They're kinda worried about her."

"Is everything okay now?" I asked. "Is Iz okay?"

He looked at me but didn't answer. I guess that *was* his answer.

He finally said, "Deputy Anderson is taking care of . . . you know, the mess in the parking lot. Everybody else is heading home. Your grandma said to tell you she'd meet you at the truck in a few minutes. She went downstairs to finish cleaning up the food."

I nodded and he fist-bumped me. "Coach wants to meet you. Said you hauled Linnea out of there like some all-star running back carrying a pigskin on fire."

"Yeah, I'm an all-star something, all right."

Kenny turned and started walking away, but Linnea suddenly shimmied down his back and ran over to me.

She held out the winning ticket for purple fourteen. It was all bent-up and crumpled from being clutched in her fist. I was pretty sure it was snotted up, too. "You want your ticket back now?"

"Nah, kid, I already got a new bike. I want you to have it."

She nodded. "Thank you, Bank-Robber Boy." And she walked away holding Kenny's hand.

I hung back awhile after they left, figuring maybe by the time I hit the parking lot, most everybody would have cleared out. But I didn't want Gram to have to come looking for me, so I finally headed to the truck at a fast trot. The parking lot was almost empty, but Gram wasn't there yet.

I still hadn't gotten over how people in the boonies

never bothered to lock their car doors. I mean, if they were anything like Gram, they left the doors to their houses standing wide-open too. I guess to make it easier for the ax murderers to get inside. But this time that lack of safety first was working to my advantage; the truck wasn't locked. I slid into the passenger seat and closed the door.

Something crinkled as I settled onto the seat. I reached under my butt and pulled out a wrinkled-up piece of paper. The first side I saw had this weird drawing. It took me a minute, but I finally figured out it was a map—of the island! That jagged-topped stump, Fingers-to-Heaven or whatever goofy name Iz had given it, jumped right off the page at me. Not far away was a big *X*. Was this somebody's idea of a joke?

But then I turned the map over. It was covered with words made from cut-out newspaper letters, like a project I had made for Mother's Day in first grade.

Or like ransom notes in those old movies.

I read it through once, straining to make out the words in the falling darkness. Then I reached over and locked the doors, one at a time because the truck was the old-school type without automatic locks.

I read the note again:

I know you have the $$$.
Bury it on the island within 24
hours. Location marked on map.
Do it or you'll be SORRy!

CHAPTER 15

It grew steadily darker as I sat there with the note in my hand. I shivered despite the fact that the windows were all rolled up and it had just turned July. The note had to be a joke, right?

Although the photo of a hunting rifle glued below the words made it hard not to take the whole thing seriously. Somebody was after me.

Suddenly the door handle rattled. I about jumped through the ceiling of the truck. When I could breathe again, I looked over and saw Gram gesturing at the lock. I stuffed the note into my back pocket and then leaned over and unlocked her door.

I could see Gram's puzzled look when the overhead light turned on. "Is something wrong, Travis? Why were the doors locked?"

"Just habit, you know, coming from a big city and all."

Gram started up the truck, but then we just sat there for a moment. She seemed to be thinking hard about something. I suppose it was my perfect chance to tell her about the note. But I knew the first thing she'd do would be to call up Deputy Dude. And I wasn't ready for another one of his friendly little chats.

Finally Gram turned to me. "That was impressive, the way you took care of Linnea. Did you get her back to her family okay?"

I nodded.

"She and Isabella have certainly had to grapple with more than any child should." Gram shook her head. "And the ticket Linnea had—was that really your winning ticket?"

I shrugged. "You already bought me that bike, so, you know, I thought . . ." I let my voice trail off. I hoped she wasn't upset that I had handed off my prize.

Gram suddenly grinned. "The look on Milo's face —oh, my heavens—when he realized you of all people had won his precious bike. That look alone was worth ten times the ticket price!"

And then she started to laugh. And once she got

going, she couldn't seem to stop. She just kept laughing, harder and harder. I swear, if she'd been in the school cafeteria drinking milk, cow juice would have been squirting out of her nose at that point.

After a while I looked around. Was I being Punk'd? But nobody jumped out of the bushes with a camera or anything.

Finally Gram took off her glasses and pulled a Kleenex out of her sleeve to wipe her eyes. "Oh, I'm so glad you decided to come see me this summer. I haven't laughed like that in years." Then she drove home in complete silence, except for an occasional laughing snort.

When we got home, I told Gram I was tired and headed straight for my bedroom. I knew I needed to come up with a plan to deal with the note, but everything that had happened in the past couple of days was starting to crash in on me. I decided to just drop into a coma and figure it all out in the morning. But I bumped my toe on something as I was pulling off my T-shirt. I looked down and there it was: the Father Box.

I hauled it up onto the bedspread and sat down on the middle of the bed. I was still feeling pretty crappy about snooping through Gram's house; there was a part of me that thought I should just put it back under her bed without looking at it any further.

But if all of this junk was about my father, didn't I have the right to look at it? It was part of who I was, whether anybody wanted me to know about it or not.

I piled everything from the box into little stacks around me, half sorting it based on what the stuff seemed to be. I ended up with an ancient photo album, a couple of yearbooks, the yellowed newspaper clippings, and a bunch of other loose papers.

I looked through the loose papers first, to see if I could find a recent address or anything similar. But it was clear everything was pretty old; the only addresses were on some letters from various army bases, which were definitely pre-robbery.

I opened the top letter and read the first several lines:

Dear Mom,

I've only been here for two weeks, but I can already tell you that all the terrible things they say about boot camp are true. But I'm not complaining (and please don't take it personally)—it's great to be anywhere but there! I miss you and I worry about Carl, but the building where I bunk holds probably twice as many people as the whole population back home. I'm finally starting to meet the world!

Farther down in the stack was a report card for John Stoiska, fifth grade. He had gotten an A in arithmetic; guess his math-genius genes hadn't made it to me.

I cracked open a yearbook and randomly flipped through it, finally turning to the index at the back. *Stoiska, John*, followed by a long list of pages. I opened to page sixty-two; there was this photo of two guys with big cheesy grins, both in football jerseys, hamming it up for the camera—and right away I knew which one was him. It was weird; it was like looking in one of those fun-house mirrors. I could see myself in him, but everything was just a little bit off. Especially the dorky hair.

The long-ago dad was holding up his fingers behind the head of the guy next to him, doing those devil horns. And I did a double take when my eyes skimmed down to read the caption: "Seniors John Stoiska and Kyle Anderson."

Kyle Anderson? Had Deputy Dude been friends with my father? You'd think maybe the big bad arm of the law could have cut me some slack for old times' sake, right? But I guess that isn't how it works: cops and robbers are sworn enemies, just like jocks and skaters or the Celtics and the Lakers.

Finally I turned to the newspaper articles. First in the stack was the front page of an old October issue of the *Prairie Press*, which I recognized as the local paper. Staring at me was the photo of my dad in his military getup and the headline "Local Link to Northern Bank Heist" plastered in big letters across the top. I started reading:

> FBI Special Agent Mark Tosch confirmed this morning that 23-year-old John Stoiska, a local resident who has been missing since his boat was found washed up the morning of September 2, is wanted for questioning in a burglary of the Community Trust Bank located in Crookston, Minnesota. The burglary likely happened sometime in the late-night hours between 9:00 p.m. on August 31, when a nearby storeowner locked up, and 8:00 a.m. on September 1, when the break-in was discovered by bank manager Vernon Coop.
>
> "This is the first time the bank has been burglarized in its seventy-five-year history," stated Coop.
>
> Authorities won't reveal what evidence they have linking Stoiska to the crime but have asked citizens to step forward with any information they have about him. Several local witnesses saw Stoiska here in town

on the day after the burglary, but he was reported missing and possibly drowned the next morning after his boat was discovered adrift. An extensive search of the lake at that time revealed no sign of Stoiska's body.

"He was a wild one, but I never figured him for a crook," said Florence Halvorsen, a waitress who served Stoiska his lunch on September 1. "Always a good tipper, too."

Authorities searched Stoiska's residence and questioned his mother, Lois Stoiska, along with several other local residents.

It appears the burglary required electrical skills and explosives. Stoiska's military service records reveal he had specialized training in those areas. In the weeks prior to the burglary, Stoiska had also spent time at a construction job near Crookston.

Authorities have stated that Stoiska was not working alone.

"The time frame and the skill level required to break into the bank and then into the vault make it highly likely that this crime required more than one perpetrator," stated Tosch. "We believe John Stoiska had at least one accomplice, and we are proceeding accordingly."

Neither authorities nor Coop would reveal the amount of money stolen, but bank sources confirmed that the timing of the heist seemed carefully planned for a maximum potential take.

A $15,000 reward has been offered for information that leads to an arrest.

There were more newspapers, but I figured it was going to take me a couple of months just to wrap my head around everything in this one article. An accomplice? Iz and Kenny and I had talked about that, but this made it seem real—there actually might be someone out there besides my father who knew what had happened that long-ago night. What exactly did all this mean? Just what evidence did the FBI have against my dad, and how come it took longer than a month for them to link him to the robbery if they had something solid?

And I had other questions too. Like, was some bank-robbing bad guy growing inside him that whole time he was getting As in fifth-grade math? Was it just waiting for its chance to leap out, like when the creature in that movie *Alien* suddenly burst out of the guy's chest?

Was it waiting there somewhere inside me, too?

Something crinkled as I shifted on the bed. I pulled the anonymous note out of my pocket and set it between the newspapers and the yearbook. Were there any real clues buried in these little piles of stuff? I couldn't see how anything here was going to lead me to the whereabouts of the person Gram had lost and I was trying to find. Maybe these pieces of junk were just the last reminders anyone would ever have of my dad.

I tried to keep my eyes open long enough to read more, but suddenly I was way too tired to resist giving in to sleep. I curled up on top of all the mess and just let myself sink into the deep waters. But right before drowning, I had one of those strange, random thoughts that sometimes happen as you go under for the last time. By showing up in town, I had become a constant reminder of my dad. All I had to do was figure out who didn't like being reminded.

CHAPTER 16

When I woke up, the wind was howling outside and rain was hammering onto the roof. I had all these questions popcorning around in my brain, heated up by my looking through the Father Box the night before. I started searching for some answers on my phone, but pretty quickly the smell of real bacon won out. The new health-conscious Ma tried to pass off some fried tofu crap called "fakon" on me, but, I mean, really? Really, Ma? So once again I threw the box back together and pushed it under my bed, stuffing the cut-and-paste note back into my pocket.

"Kenny called. He said you should come over if you want to play some kind of video game. He seemed fairly excited about it. I think it's nice you've made a friend so quickly. Kenny's a good boy." Gram plopped some slices of bacon next to some eggs and set them in front of me at the table.

"Thanks." I had lots of questions for Gram, too. I was determined to finally make her give me some answers, but I decided to test the waters first.

"Uh, Gram, that deputy guy who was here—he seemed to kind of feel at home."

Gram gave me a surprised look, but then her eyes did that thing people's eyes do when they go all vague and unfocused and you know they're seeing something nobody else in the room can see. "He and your father grew up together. They were best friends, really, in high school. Kyle Anderson was over here more times than I can count when he was a teenager."

She took a sip from her coffee mug. "The two of them were unlikely friends. You couldn't overlook John, but people never took much notice of Kyle. Until John took him under his wing. I was proud of John for that, for going out of his way to befriend somebody who so clearly needed a friend. Kyle was so serious—I think things were hard for him at home, although he wouldn't talk about it—and John got him to lighten up. I always hoped that it might work the other way too, that he might be a steadying influence for John."

Gram pushed her plate away from her; she hadn't eaten half of her breakfast. "That isn't how it turned out, of course. It seems their friendship was another thing that got away from your father. After all, Kyle was on a path to becoming the town's deputy, and John ended up becoming our most notorious law-breaker. That's too much of a divide for any friendship to stand."

It was only my first question, and it had already put this look onto Gram's face that made her seem old. I mean, even older than usual.

Someday, maybe I would get up the courage to push past the sad in her face and just ask her my hardest questions. Maybe I'd even try asking Ma one more time — I mean, it wasn't as if she'd robbed a sperm bank to come up with me, right? She'd spent at least enough time with the guy who'd donated my Y-chromosome to create a lifetime souvenir; she must have known something about who he really was.

But that look on Gram's face meant I was done with twenty questions for the morning. I kept my mouth shut and stared out at the lake. The sky was as gray and stormy as my insides.

Gram stood and picked up our plates. "It seemed

to me that Kyle was much too hard on you when he came to ask about the bank money the other day, but I've been thinking about that. I suppose I didn't account for the fact that he probably still feels . . . very betrayed that his good friend committed such a serious crime. I imagine he feels he can't trust this family anymore. It's not fair to you, but life so seldom is fair."

I nodded and headed for the bathroom, anxious to shower off the bad feeling that was dogging me after our talk, but it didn't work. So I was eager to head next door to Kenny's. He answered my knock and led me to a family room. Most of the surfaces held hairbrushes or stuffed animals or pink-colored items. Kenny waved his hand at the TV.

"Yo, we got the game room to ourselves! Never happens around here."

I raised my eyebrows and he continued. "Most of 'em have gone off to get Linnea her bike. The kid wouldn't shut up about it; she talked more than I've ever heard her talk in her life. I think Iz is still asleep and Kari's probably working."

It should have been the perfect time to haul the first-grade cut-and-glue project out of my pocket and ask Kenny what he thought I should do about the anonymous note, but I held back. The past few days I'd bounced from one emo crisis to the next. Ever since Gram had told me that Kenny had called that morning, I'd been hoping he and I shared the same gaming taste. And after the talk I'd had with Gram that morning, I especially needed to just lose myself for a while in some relaxing fun that featured bloodthirsty killer zombies or maniacal Nazis—anything easier to stomach than what was going on in my real life.

We were having a great time shooting at each other when the air changed and I looked up. Iz had walked into the room.

"Gotcha!" said Kenny. I'd lost the game.

Iz had her arms folded tightly across her chest, and she had this kind of crazy-eyed look I'd seen once on Jason Kalooky's dog when it had gotten hit by a car. The dog turned out okay—the vet had fixed him right up and he got along great with just three legs.

I wasn't so convinced that Iz was going to survive her own personal car wreck.

But Kenny didn't seem to notice how she looked. "The boss is here," he said to me. "Fun's over. We gotta get back to work and find that money."

Iz turned those crazy eyes on him. "You made it

clear enough last night that hanging out with me isn't your first choice. You don't need to tell me again that I'm no fun."

"Chill—it was just a joke. And what are you even talking about? What'd I do last night?" he asked.

"I'm talking about the fact that Cody Svengrud treats me like crap but you couldn't move fast enough to go sit at his table. And I'm talking about the fact that you're constantly complaining because I asked you to spend just a little of your precious time helping me out. Well, you'll be superglad to know that I don't care about the money anymore. So go play with your brain-dead football friends all you want. Knock yourself out. Kill whatever brain cells you have left."

I had always thought that phrases like "his jaw dropped" or "his eyes narrowed" were just expressions, but I swear, Kenny's jaw about hit the carpet and his eyes turned into slits.

"Whaddya mean you don't care about the money?"

"I mean that I. Don't. Care. I don't care about finding the stupid money and I don't care who's out there spending it and I especially don't care what you do with your stupid self the rest of the stupid summer. I don't care!"

Kenny hulked to his feet. It was easy to forget how big he was because he was usually so laid-back, but I could suddenly see why the other team had something to fear when he strapped on the shoulder pads.

"You don't care?" he yelled. "You don't care that you blackmailed me into following you around for the entire month of June? You don't care that I've wasted a whole month of summer football trying to help you out? You don't care?"

This was turning out to be a bloodier battle than the game I'd just lost. Apparently, the fact that they were cousins forced to fight over the same bathroom had turned them into something like über-siblings. I gotta admit, it was freaking me out a little bit. It was one of those things about being an only child: I'd never really gotten used to the way brothers and sisters go for the jugular when they fight, even though I'd seen it in action more than once at Kalooky's house. I mean, pit bulls or Mean Girls ain't got nothing on that kind of death match.

And neither Iz nor Kenny seemed to even remember I was in the room. I looked down at myself to make sure that Jesus hadn't delivered on that invisibility thing half a day too late.

"I knew it!" said Iz. "I knew that the only reason you were willing to spend any time with the freak girl is that I bribed you to do it. So you should be happy that I'm setting you free. You can quit worrying your poor little brain over freaky Isabella and her sad freaky family mess and go back to living your perfect little life with your perfect little family and your perfect idiot friends."

"Say, Self-Absorbed, maybe you wouldn't get called a freak so often if you got your head out of your butt long enough to notice you aren't the only one with problems!" If his voice ratcheted any louder, it was going to go beyond the level where human ears could hear it.

"What's that supposed to mean?" asked Iz. Her voice was low and deadly; right then, I wasn't sure which of them was more dangerous.

"It means that I get that your life stinks. It stinks like *Snakes on a Plane* stank. But that doesn't mean that you get to ignore that everybody else has crap too. I mean, I may be dumb, but I'm not so stupid that I didn't catch on to how you've called me an idiot in one way or another five times in the last five minutes," said Kenny.

I couldn't sit still any longer; I got up and walked over to stare out the window. There seemed to be fewer white-topped waves on the lake, and the rain had stopped.

Kenny kept going. "You think I like being reminded I'm too dumb to pass a test without cheating off my cousin? You think my life feels easy when the only thing I do really good is throw a football, and then they threaten to take that away because my loser brain can't read right? You think my life's so perfect? You try living it for five minutes. Maybe if you thought about somebody besides yourself for one second, you'd find out it's just as hard to be stupid Kenny as it is to be freaky Iz."

Iz's voice suddenly fell to a whisper. I had to turn back around to really hear her. "Oh, touché, Kenny. You got me good with that one. And just so you know, *that's* what *touché* really means." And then she dropped onto the couch as if she'd been sliced in half by a shotgun blast. She collapsed in on herself and started crying like I'd never seen anybody cry. As soon as she let loose with the bawling, Kenny got this look on his face as if he'd been kicked where it counts.

Suddenly Jen stormed into the room and let fly with the ultimate mother weapon: she middle-named him. "Kenneth James Nelson, Jr., what on earth is going on in here? We could hear you yelling from outside!" She swooped over to the couch and scooped up Iz, settling back down with Iz cradled in her lap as if she were no bigger than Linnea.

Jen looked at us over the top of Iz's head, and now her voice just sounded tired. "Why don't you boys go outside and look at the new bike."

See, there was another reason life stinks when you're thirteen: you can still remember the once-upon-a-time when a new bike could fix almost anything, but by thirteen you've been kicked where it counts enough times to know there just isn't going to be any happily-ever-after.

We hurried outside like it was a school fire drill during a math test; I had to admit, I was secretly relieved a grownup had gotten home in time to clean up the carnage.

I wasn't sure if Kenny even remembered I was there until we hit the front porch and he turned to me.

"Yo," he said. "Awkward. Sorry."

"'S'all right," I answered. "But I gotta ask you something. You don't have to answer if you don't want to, but I gotta ask."

He nodded.

"What's with Iz's family? I mean, it's clear her dad's got issues, but nobody even talks about her mom. What's up with that?"

Kenny shrugged. "Aunt Deb is just . . . away. Somewhere. She needed a time-out or something. She turned up here about three months ago with the girls, and she talked to Mom for a while, and then she just left—without Iz and Linnea. Mom had to tell them she was gone."

For just a moment I got this guilty feeling about my ma; I mean, I had pretty much taken off on her with no warning too.

Kenny kept going. "And their dad, he's been kind of in and out for a while—more out, really—and it's pretty clear he can't take care of them. I mean, showing up every few weeks to play the town drunk won't win him any father-of-the-year medals, you know? So they're, like, borrowing my parents for a while. It stinks for them—I mean, I really do get that it's worse than anything I have going on. It's just that once in a while Iz makes me crazy mad, and I say things I don't really mean . . . You know, Aunt Deb sends her these post cards. They always say she'll come home soon.

But there's no address where Iz can go see her. And even if she came back today . . . I mean, will Iz ever be able to forget she left in the first place? What could she even say to her mom after she took off like that?"

He was asking the wrong guy. I was piling up those same questions about my father, and instead of finding any answers, I just seemed to think of more questions.

It was like having to take a multiple-choice test you know you can't ever pass; as much as I kept turning it over in my head, I couldn't come up with an answer I liked.

Q: Which dad did I want most?

A: Dead Dad?

B: Never-Even-Wanted-to-Meet-Me Dad?

C: Selfishly-Letting-Me-Take-the-Rap-for-Spending-the-Bank-Money Dad?

I wanted a test with one more option:

D: None of the above.

Just then Linnea came running up. "Look! Look what I got!" She shot us a missing-toothed, jack-o'-lantern grin, waving and pointing at the new bike. It was purple, of course. Big Ken was tightening some screws on it, and then he stood up and handed the bike over to her. When he saw Kenny, he gave him this look and hooked him with his finger over to the other side of the driveway. I decided I had probably long over-stayed my welcome, but just as I was turning to head back to Gram's, Linnea pedaled over and skidded to a stop in front of me.

"Watch!" she commanded. "See how fast I can go!" The bossy attitude she pulled out just then kind of reminded me of her sister, so I sat down in the wet grass and watched.

Krissy was riding around too, on her pink bike, and both girls' ponytails were streaming out from under their helmets as they rode through the puddles the rain had left behind. And Kenny and Big Ken were having this obvious man-to-man, with lots of hand gesturing and guilty looks on Kenny's part and lots of nodding and earnest concern and back slapping from Big Ken.

I guess they got it all worked out, because Kenny ducked into the garage and came out with a football. The two of them started throwing it back and forth to each other in the yard, just a father and son tossing the old pigskin around on a now-perfect summer day —I swear, the sun came out at that exact moment and shone down on the whole picture.

Watching it from the sidelines was like watching one of those old movies from back when they had first invented color film, where everything looks a little too blue or a little too pink or a little too yellow. My brain just couldn't buy into this world; its colors were too far off from the colors I was used to.

Then Iz came outside and sat down next to me, raising her arm to wave as Linnea flashed by on her bike.

"Thank you for giving her the winning ticket," Iz said, looking straight ahead. "It's the best thing that's happened to her in a really long time."

Part of me wanted her to go on thinking I was the sort of guy who was naturally kind to children and small animals, but there was this other part of me that felt as if I had to tell her the truth, even though I didn't always see the need to do that with anybody else. Turns out that part of me also had a really big mouth, because it blurted out, "I didn't need it. I mean, I'm glad she got the bike, but I've already got one. So I didn't need the ticket."

"That's okay. Still," she said, and then she let her hand kind of slip down so it rested right next to mine, barely touching, but touching enough so that every-thing suddenly shifted for me, like when you're look-ing through a kaleidoscope and you give it one small turn and suddenly the colors fall into a whole new pat-tern you've never seen before.

CHAPTER 17

We sat like that for a while, not talking or anything. I think I was pretty much not even breathing. Finally Iz turned and looked at me. I could tell she'd been crying again.

But mostly what I noticed was that the evil fairy was gone. Totally AWOL.

And when she had the evil fairy on tap, I was a little bit afraid of Iz. But without the evil fairy there to guard her, I was a little bit afraid *for* Iz.

"So," she said, "you just came over to play video games with Kenny, and instead you ended up in the middle of my family's mess . . ."

"That's okay." I decided I needed to make her smile. "I'm tough. I can handle the rough stuff. You saw how I faced down that butter head without flinching."

She did smile a little but it faded fast. "I want you to understand. Money—that was such a big problem around my house. My parents were always fighting about it, and I guess I figured if I could come up with enough somehow, maybe then . . . But after last night, I finally just get it. Money can't fix what's wrong with my family."

She watched Linnea zoom by again. "I remember feeling like that. Like I owned the summer. When I was little, back when my dad . . ." She gulped. "I still called him 'Daddy' then. He used to put me up on his shoulders and polka the two of us through the flower gardens. My mom would yell, 'Don't you go trampling those asters, Henry David,' and he'd just laugh and say, 'I'm looking for a place to plant this sweet pea of mine.'"

She got quiet and I thought about her dad bulldozing over all the chicken-poop cheerleaders the night before. Somehow I couldn't picture that same guy dancing through flowers, holding his own little girl safely up high.

"And then he just . . . changed?" I asked. I was thinking about when Ma had first met my stepfather. How it seemed as if I blinked once and then everything was totally different from the way it had always been. How suddenly there was all this new stuff in place: new Ma, new boyfriend and then stepfather, new place to live, but with the same old me, who didn't fit anymore.

Iz shook her head. "Things didn't change all at once. More like bad things kept happening, until they piled up so high that they blocked out all the good. First my grandpa and then my grandma died. It was their farm we'd been living on. Mom and Aunt Jen grew up there too. Mom used to talk about how we were eating rhubarb jam from a plant that her grandma had planted. And then when my grandparents died, somehow my parents couldn't make the farm work anymore. The fights about money started. And then the drinking. Daddy didn't come home some nights. Then he'd stay away for longer and longer. Then he hardly came home at all. Finally the bank took the farm away."

I watched while she rubbed really hard at a mosquito bite on her knee with her knuckles, like making it hurt was the only way to take away the sting.

"So your mom brought you here to stay for a while?" I said.

Iz stopped her rubbing and sat perfectly still for a moment. Then her shoulders slumped and her head drooped and she leaned forward as if it was just too much effort to hold herself up any longer.

"What if it's not just for a while?" she whispered. "What if she's not coming back?"

She was still leaning forward in that broken-down way. A grownup would have probably lied and told her that everything was going to be fine. But how could I say that? The whole reason I was in Minnesota was to figure out what I could about my own dad—the one who had left one day and never came back. And so far my plan wasn't working out all that great for me.

Iz started talking again. "Aunt Jen says Mom just had to get away from here for a while, because all those bad things had happened here. That she's figuring out how we can be a family again even though everything's different now. And while she does that, she needs me and Linnea to be somewhere safe with the same schools and friends and relatives so that nothing else has to change for us." Iz sat up straight and tossed her head like she was shaking off a creepy-crawly. "But I guess she didn't really think that through—because her leaving us behind is the change I hate most of all."

I didn't know what I could say to make any of that better, so I turned my hand and gave hers a little squeeze. And I meant to pull my hand away really fast after that, but instead she hung on.

"Trav, don't you miss your mom?"

I was smart enough to know we were still talking about her mom, not just my mom. So instead of snapping out the "no" that jumped to my lips, I made myself think about it.

And the truth was, I did miss my old mom. But I wasn't sure she really existed now; I was pretty sure she'd been permanently replaced with a new 2.0 version called Married Ma, a ma who didn't belong to just me anymore. A ma I didn't always recognize.

But part of the problem was, she didn't seem to recognize me anymore, either. I couldn't seem to morph into the right shape to fit in with her new happy family. I was no longer who she wanted me to be.

So I told Iz the truth again. "She proved that what

I want doesn't really matter. I was just supposed to fall into line with all her changes because I'm the kid. I'm still too mad at her to miss her. And right now all the things I'm learning here about my dad feel way more important than thinking about her and all that stuff, anyway."

Iz thought about that for a minute and then nodded. "I want you to know I didn't mean everything I said to Kenny. I mean, I am done with the money hunt for me—but I know you still have to find the cash, to prove you haven't had it all along. And to figure out more about your dad. So I want you to know I'll still help you look."

The note in my pocket suddenly seemed to be burning through to my skin. I looked around, but everybody else had vanished while we were talking, so I reached back and pulled it out, smoothing it out on my knee.

"What's that?" Iz peered over my arm.

"I found it in the truck last night," I said. "After . . . after everything, when I was waiting for Gram to finish cleanup."

Iz leaned in a little closer to read the note, and I suddenly really needed to know if her hair still smelled of strawberries. I bent my head just to take a small sniff.

And next thing I knew, she jerked her head up and jackhammered into my chin. And I gotta say, the girl had a *hard* head. Seriously, the tooth fairy was going to owe me bigtime, because I had a fortune full of loose teeth rattling around inside my skull.

I was massaging my chin, wondering what a broken jaw felt like, and Iz was giving me this puzzled look while she rubbed the top of her skull. I wasn't sure if the look was because she'd read the note or because she had caught me sniffing and was trying to figure out when I'd turned into a golden retriever.

She finally repeated the end of the note in this low voice and pointed at the cut-out gun. "'Or you'll be sorry'? Trav, this is kind of scary. Have you shown anybody else?"

"I was waiting to show you first," I said, and I realized as I spoke that it was true. "I'm hoping it's just somebody's stupid idea of a joke. I was thinking that maybe that Svengrud kid made it—he seems to have it in for me."

"Cody?" Iz looked over the note again. "I don't

know. He's pretty in-your-face. This secret-note thing doesn't seem like his style."

I shrugged, but she was right. It was tempting to blame somebody I already hated, but the note writer could be anybody.

"Maybe . . . maybe you better show it to Deputy Anderson," Iz said. "I mean, if somebody is making threats against you, that's the kind of thing he should know, right?"

I shook my head. "That guy thinks I'm as big a troublemaker as my father was—he can't see me as anything but bad news. Gram even admitted earlier that he just doesn't trust our family. Besides, he's another one who thinks I have the stolen money. If I show him the note, he'll just use it as an excuse to hammer me with more pointless questions about where I've got the money stashed."

"So what are you going to do? It's not like you can bury money you don't have," Iz said.

"Yeah, there's that," I agreed. "For a while I thought I'd just ignore this. But now that the weather has turned better . . ." I squinted up at the sun. "I maybe have an idea. Do you think I could get Kenny to take me out to the island this afternoon?"

"I'll ask him," said Iz.

"*You'll* ask him?" I could hear the surprise in my own voice.

"Look, you hang around the two of us long enough, you'll see me and Kenny go at it again, sooner or later," she said. "That's just us. Everybody else is used to it. We've been that way since we were babies. One time when we were eight, he got so mad that he set my Barbies on fire. We both get real mad, but afterward, we're always buds again."

Me and Ma seemed to have a permanent "mad" on. It was hard for me to picture getting over a fight that easily.

"Travis, lunchtime." Gram was waving at me from her yard next door. I stuffed the note back into my pocket and stood up.

"But what do you want to do on the island?" Iz asked.

"I'm still working it out," I said. "But I'm hoping I'll know when we get there."

CHAPTER 18

I had scarfed down three tuna melts by the time Iz called to tell me Kenny was up for a cruise as soon as they finished lunch. I cleared the table and then asked Gram if I could borrow some scissors, glue, and a blank piece of paper to make a card for Ma. I didn't think Gram bought it, but I guess she figured I couldn't get myself into too much trouble with those items. I mean, what diabolical scheme could I be up to? A fight-to-the-death game of rock-paper-scissors?

Rather than make her any more suspicious, I waited until she wasn't looking before sneaking an old newspaper out of the recycling bin and a plastic bag out of the drawer. Fortunately my father's old Monopoly game was stored on a shelf in his room, so I'd already gotten what I needed out of there. I'd also nabbed the newspaper article that explained the cops' theory on how the whole thing went down and pointed the finger at my father. I grabbed a shovel out of the shed and hauled everything else in a paper bag to Kenny's boat.

Iz was right; somehow she and Kenny had made up. They weren't going to win a Nobel Peace Prize or anything, though; it was more like after the Stanley Cup finals, when players who had pummeled one another bloody on the ice still lined up to shake hands.

"Righteous—did ya bring snacks?" asked Kenny once we got to the island, gesturing to the bag I was holding.

You gotta admit the guy was consistent with his priorities. I pulled out the cookies Gram had handed me as I'd headed out the door.

"Score!" said Kenny, digging in.

Iz watched while I emptied out the rest of the bag onto Fairy Rock. "Is this for what I think it's for?" she asked, grabbing a piece of newspaper just as a gust of wind started to whip it away.

"What's that?" Kenny mumbled around the entire cookie he had just shoved into his mouth as I pulled the cut-and-paste note out of my pocket. I set it on top of the other stuff, weighing it down with a small rock so it wouldn't blow off.

"Somebody really wants me to give up the bank cash I don't actually have," I told him. "They sent me this little love letter asking me to pretty please hand it over."

Kenny picked up the note and read slowly; I couldn't help but remember what he'd said about his reading problems and wondered if the alphabet-soup approach with all the cut-out letters was giving him even more trouble than usual. But eventually he set the note back under the rock and said, "Bro, that's just cold."

"Since you don't have the money, you're going to write a note back and bury that instead?" Iz asked.

I nodded. "Somebody wants to play chicken with me, so I guess I'll play chicken. Only way to see how serious they are. And my chicken-poop-bingo win kind of proves the chickens are on my side, right?"

"So what are you going to say?" Kenny picked up the shovel and rammed the tip of it into the sand. "Maybe just put the word *psych* in big letters? Or 'Gotcha, loser'?"

"Nah, I'll be polite. I'm gonna say, 'I don't have

a clue where the stupid money is, but if you find it, please feel free to stick it up your—'"

"Okay, I get where you're going here," Iz interrupted. "Look, Trav, if this is just some idiot having fun, then I agree it's tempting to yank his chain. But in case this is somehow a real threat, you don't want to tick him off, right?"

I didn't know—I thought I was pretty much okay with ticking him off at this point.

"Hey—I've got it," said Kenny. "Once the note is buried, let's hide out here on the island until the bad guy shows up to find it. Then we'll nab him!"

I watched Iz open and then close her mouth. I could tell she'd instantly seen the problem with Kenny's plan and just as quickly decided not to be the one to point out the flaw in his thinking.

"You know the note writer will circle the island first to see if somebody's already out here. Once he sees your boat, he'll give up and come back after we're gone," I said.

Kenny thought a moment longer. "If we were all half-fish like Iz, we could swim out here. Then there wouldn't be the boat to give us away."

I shook my head at him. "I know I can't bring it

like Iz." I shook my head at her, too. "And before you say you'll swim out by yourself to play girl detective, uh-uh. This guy really could mean business."

Iz shrugged, but I could tell she was seriously considering the Nancy Drew thing. Then she said, "Aunt Jen has really good binoculars for bird watching. I guess we could spy on the island from home, and circle around it in Kenny's boat once in a while, to see who shows up with a shovel."

"If he's smart, he'll wait until dark, but I think that's the best we can do," I said. "And if we do miss him, I've got another idea for bringing this guy into the open."

I handed Iz the anonymous note. "Try to figure out this map he's drawn. I think this thing sticking up here is Fingers-to-Heaven. I can't make sense of the rest of it. But you know every rock and piece of driftwood on this place."

I sat down next to Fairy Rock, using it like a craft table while I went to work with the scissors and glue. Kenny and Iz bent their heads together over the map and then wandered off into the trees, their voices drifting back even though I couldn't see them anymore.

They returned to the beach as I was gluing on the

final letter. "I'm pretty sure we know where X marks the spot. You about ready?" Iz asked.

I handed her the note. Then I pushed to my feet and pulled the Monopoly money out of my pocket, pretending to fan it the way bigtime rollers in Vegas always do in the movies. "We'll just wrap it around this funny money, stick it into the plastic bag, and bury it."

Iz looked over what I'd written and she frowned. Then she read it aloud for Kenny's sake. "'Here's a down payment. If you want to talk about the other cash my father left behind, we need to do that in person.'"

"Touché!" said Kenny. I cut my eyes to Iz but she wasn't paying any attention to him, just staring at my note.

"I don't know, Trav," she said slowly. "I really think you're asking for it."

I shrugged. "Whatever. I need to know who I'm dealing with, and this is the only thing I can think of to draw him out."

"Kind of like a draw in football, right? Fake him out and then make him play the game your way instead of his." Kenny picked up the shovel and led us past Fingers-to-Heaven to the spot they'd decided was the *X* on the map. "Let's get this sucker into the ground. How deep you wanna go?" He started go-phering down with the shovel, heaping up a pile of dirt in record time.

"I'd say make him dig to China, but what's the point? We want him to find it before Christmas, right?" I slipped the note and Monopoly money into the plastic bag and dropped it into the hole. "That's good enough."

Iz and I watched while Kenny piled the dirt back into place even faster than he'd dug it out. Then we trailed back to the beach.

"Whoa, sunstroke—I gotta rest a minute, man." Kenny collapsed spread-eagle onto the sand with a big sigh as if I really *had* made him dig to Beijing. He threw his arm over his eyes to shade them.

I pulled out the bag of now-almost-gone cookies and sat down with my back against Fairy Rock.

"So." Iz plopped down next to me. "You really think this is a good idea?"

I shrugged and looked over at Kenny. My own head was feeling a little dizzy; I didn't know if it was from the glare or from all the maybes that kept swirl-ing through my mind.

"I've been thinking a lot about it." I handed Iz the bag of cookies. "But I can't figure out if the note writer is somehow a part of the whole bank robbery or if the note's just somebody's idea of a sick joke or one of those fake-outs you see in mystery stories."

Iz swallowed a bite of cookie. "Red herrings, you mean?"

"Yeah, red herrings. Something that seems important but just distracts you from the real mystery. I mean, the real mystery is, did my dad really rob the bank, and if so, is he the one back here spreading the loot or has somebody else gotten his hands on it? Like I was thinking, what if somebody from town actually already found the money, but wanted to keep the whole big bunch of it and not just settle for the little reward? And when I turned up, it looked like the perfect chance to safely start spending the cash because I would be blamed."

Kenny let out this snort, but with his eyes hidden behind his arm, I couldn't tell if he was questioning my reasoning or if it was just some weird kind of snoring.

I brushed cookie crumbs off my hands and reached into the paper bag again, pulling out the yellowed newspaper article about the bank break-in.

"I was reading some of this stuff from that box you found under Gram's bed." I handed Iz the clipping. "You were right when you talked about my dad having an accomplice. Maybe the accomplice wrote the note."

Iz took the last bite of her cookie and looked back and forth from the newspaper photo of my dad in his military uniform to me a couple times. Maybe she was seeing that thing people kept mentioning—how much we looked alike?

"Or this note writer could be somebody who's been looking for the money all these years and never found it, so he's trying to spook me into giving it up," I said. "I mean, think how mad you were when you first met me, 'cause you thought I had come here to ace you out of the reward."

Iz's cheeks turned a little pink but she nodded. "That's why I don't know if it's such a good idea to answer him back like you did." She reached out and placed her hand on my forearm. I had thought the sun was hot, but this was a whole different kind of warm. "Are you sure you want to leave that note? There's still time to dig it up again."

"Even if the accomplice is just one of the

possibilities for the note writer, I can't miss the chance to connect with him," I said.

"But if it is the accomplice, doesn't that guarantee he's dangerous?" Iz asked.

I tapped the newspaper. "It says in here that it was a bank *burglary*, not a bank robbery. I Googled them this morning because I didn't know the difference. Robbers break in when there are people around, waving guns and stuff. Burglars, they do their thing at night, when nobody's around to get hurt. I don't think this note writer really wants to hurt anybody. I think he just wants to scare me. Once he finds out I'm not going to scare that easily, maybe he'll have to come talk to me. That's my chance to find out more about my dad."

Kenny suddenly sat straight up and blinked at the two of us. "We better get our butts out of here. Like you said, the bad guy's not gonna show while he can see the good guys' boat on shore."

Iz dropped her hand and I looked over at her worried face. "Yeah, time to go," I said. I mean, us macho guys, we had to play it cool around the girls, even if we were a little freaked, right? But when Kenny got up and walked away to pull the anchor out of the sand, I reached over to nudge Iz's hand with mine.

"I just have to know," I said, too low for Kenny to hear. "The accomplice is the only one other than my dad who knows what really went down, right? If there's a chance there's somebody out there who knows the truth about my father, I have to do whatever I can to find out."

Iz nodded at me once again. But the worry didn't leave her face the whole time we bounced back home. She just stared toward the island where we had left the Monopoly money and the note waiting for whoever was going to show up to pass Go and collect the $200.

CHAPTER 19

The more freaked Iz looked, the more stoked I got. I could just tell that something was going to go down soon. Maybe I'd called somebody's bluff. Or maybe I'd set myself up for the big chicken in the sky to squirt green poop all over the bingo square I happened to find myself standing on at that moment. But at least I was taking some action instead of waiting around to get punked. I was sure that we'd be able to nail the note writer and find out what he knew about my dad.

When we hit shore, Kenny ran up to his house to find the binoculars. Iz and I were supposed to keep watch over the island.

Iz stared out at the water. "So besides not really knowing who you might be messing with, there's this other thing . . . Trav, sometimes parents, they . . . they just aren't who you need them to be." She turned to watch me bounce around on the dock, working off a sudden adrenaline buzz. "Have you thought what it could do to you if you find out something about your father you don't want to hear?"

Like, for instance, that he was a bank robber? Too late—she'd already let that cat out of the bag my first morning in town. But I decided to cut her some slack; after all, she had to be walking a minefield for me here, being willing to talk about parents who let you down. I mean, just look at the source of her own chromosomal soup.

But I couldn't let anything or anyone—including Iz and her worries—stop me. I'd come to the End of Nowhere determined to learn "the whole truth and nothing but the truth" about my old man. So even though it was turning into one of those "be careful what you wish for" moments in life, I had to keep going. So what if the final package of facts pretty much bit the big one? I'd still be learning about the guy who'd contributed to my DNA but not my college fund. And I could handle the truth. Whatever it was. Right?

In the end, hadn't I proved I could pull off that walking-catfish thing? When the water in the

California pond had started to feel toxic . . . no problem, I just moved myself along. Same went for here—if it turned out Daddy-O had made choices that left me high and dry in Minnesota, then I would just move myself along again, testing out ponds until I found one that I could call home.

Funny thing was, despite all the crap that kept getting dumped onto my head, I was starting to really like the Minnesota pond. Iz and Kenny and Gram all seemed to have their own way of helping me feel like this was where I belonged. So I hoped the pond wouldn't have to dry up too soon.

I stopped bouncing. "Whatever I find out about my dad, I'll be okay—I promise you." I paused, trying to figure out how to say it. "And you know, I'm, uh . . . sorry. About your mom and your dad and all that stuff that you're going through. I know how it must be for you."

She jerked a shoulder in acknowledgment. Then she turned away to look out over the lake.

Her head suddenly whipped back around to me. "There's a boat pulling up to the island. Where's Kenny?"

Right then he came out holding the binoculars

and a sandwich. Iz grabbed the binoculars away from him. "What took you so long, other than stopping to fill that endless pit you call a stomach?"

"The binoculars weren't in the house, so I figured they were in one of the cars. But I had to wait because Dad was in the garage. If he saw me plowing through all that crap in the van, he'd get it into his head I should clean the whole thing out. *Then* where would you be when you needed my help to catch the bad guy?"

Iz let out something of a snarl and kept adjusting the eyepieces. Kenny looked out toward the lake for the first time since returning. "Hey, a boat's pulled up on the island."

"Really, Mr. Observant?" Iz dropped the binoculars from her eyes and sighed. "False alarm. It's Jill Iverson and that college boyfriend of hers. They're just out there to — " She stopped abruptly and her eyes shot around to me. I'd never seen anyone go red that fast.

It didn't take a brain surgeon to guess what Jill and her boyfriend were up to. I felt my face go instantly hot.

"What? Lemme see." Kenny grabbed the binoculars away from Iz and raised them to his own eyes. "Whoa! Gotta give the dude points for that move!"

"Perv!" Iz turned her back on us and folded her arms over her chest with a huff.

"Hey, you were the one to bring it up in the first place." Kenny lowered the binoculars and winked at me. "Show's over. They must have moved into the trees. I guess our bad guy will wait until their boat is gone before heading out there too, huh?"

"Probably." I nodded.

"Kenny!" I hadn't noticed Krissy and Linnea until they were standing right next to us. "What are you doing with those? Mom's gonna be mad if you're peeking at girls again."

Kenny scowled at his younger sister. "So Mom doesn't have to know, if certain bigmouths just keep their traps shut."

Krissy scowled back at him.

Linnea gave a solemn nod. "If you took us out tubing, maybe we wouldn't have time to tell your mom."

You had to give the kid credit—she'd pulled out that bit of blackmail without blinking.

Kenny shook his head. "Can't right now, Squid. I've got more important stuff to do."

Iz leaned over and punched Kenny in the arm,

then gave him an intent look. "Actually, I think that's a great idea."

Kenny looked confused, so Iz continued. "Weren't you just saying you're worried that your dad will make you clean out the van if he sees you here? And how much you'd rather spend the afternoon out on the water? Circling around the island? Watching all the other boaters come and go? Tubing would be perfect."

"Oh—oh, yeah. Yeah, that's right. Okay, everybody go put on your swimsuit and find your life jacket. And tell Mom we're taking you tubing but *don't* mention the binoculars or I'll throw you overboard." The girls scattered and Kenny looked at me. "You too, man."

Tubing at munchkin speed proved to be the perfect way to keep our eyes on the island for the rest of the afternoon without looking too obvious. Other boats zipped past us; some held people fishing, some were pulling water-skiers, and one big pontoon boat was loaded down with high school partiers. Kenny almost ran us into a sailboat while cranking his head around to check out the bikinis on board. But none of those boats landed on the island.

We had only two small glitches. The first happened

when Kenny insisted it was my turn to try tubing. I had to admit, it didn't look all that exciting as far as rides go; "three-toed sloth" seemed to be Kenny's fastest tubing speed. But Linnea wouldn't leave it alone until I agreed to go, so I tore myself away from covertly staring at Iz.

As soon as I'd settled into the tube for a relaxing cruise, Kenny cranked the engine so high that I was bouncing like crazy over the water, almost—but not quite—flying. Then the tube hit some backwash and I had to make a choice between saving the ride and saving my dignity, because it suddenly became clear that my swim shorts had maybe one more good bounce —if I was lucky. No way I was risking an early moon sighting with Iz and the little girls watching me from the boat, so I let go and made a grab for the shorts just in time, drinking about a gallon of lake water in the process and coming up for air to hear the rest of them cackling like maniacs.

The second glitch happened when we were around the other side of the island and the boat suddenly sputtered twice, coughed, and then stopped altogether.

"Uh-oh," said Linnea.

Kenny kept jiggling and unscrewing things on the

motor. Then he dropped his hands down and just sat there.

"What's the matter?" asked Linnea.

Iz sighed her biggest sigh yet and opened her mouth to say something. Kenny gave her a look and she closed it again. Then he ripped out a fart louder than anything even Kalooky could manage, and Kalooky was West Coast champion.

"It's like this, Squid," he said, over the top of Linnea's giggles. "I'm not out of gas, but the boat is."

Big Ken eventually showed up in a neighbor's boat with a gas can and an order for us to head straight home for dinner. "Come over when you're done with supper, Trav, and bring your grandma," he said. "Jen's decided we need some family time and we're building a campfire."

I kept an eye on the island as best I could during dinner, but nobody else landed on the side I could see. By the time I'd helped Gram finish the dishes, the sun was starting to sneak its way out of the sky.

I was sucking in wood smoke and competing with Kenny to see which of us could stuff the most marshmallows into our mouth at once when Kenny's mom came over and dropped down next to us.

"Stop trying to choke yourself and go burn your poor old mother a marshmallow," she told Kenny. She waited until he'd gone over to the fire and then turned to me. Fortunately that gave me time to choke down my own mouthful; it was clear she had plans to grill me about something.

"It's so good to have you here, Travis," she said. "I know your grandma loves it. And I think it's made somebody else pretty happy too."

I thought she was talking about Linnea; the kid had decided to thank me for the bike by charring me a series of increasingly sticky marshmallows. But when I followed Jen's eyes, I realized she was watching someone else instead: Iz, who was sitting across the fire with her arms curled around her upraised knees. She had this faraway look and a little I've-got-a-secret smile just at the corners of her lips.

I dropped my eyes and felt this big blush rise up my cheeks. I hoped that between the dusk and the heat of the fire, Jen wouldn't notice. She looked me over for a while without saying anything else, long enough for me to figure she'd guessed the truth. Then she chuckled and patted my knee before getting up to go pull Krissy farther back from the fire.

Eventually everybody but me, Kenny, and Iz got too full of marshmallows and too tired of swatting the buzzing mosquitoes, and they drifted inside in ones and twos.

"Fifteen minutes," said Jen, giving Kenny and Iz a look before she pulled Linnea away from me and off to bed. "Tomorrow's a big day, and I can tell you two haven't had enough sleep lately."

The three of us sat watching the fire die down into gray ash, not really saying much, but it was quiet in that good way, where you don't feel the need to mess things up with words. The full dark settled around my sunburned shoulders like a warm blanket. Somewhere in the distance a series of fireworks popped in an uneven rhythm, like when the first few kernels of popcorn start heating, and I remembered that tomorrow was the Fourth of July. Independence Day.

"Time!" Jen's voice drifted out of an upstairs window.

I watched Kenny get to his feet and poke at the dead embers with a stick.

"Gram says I have to go to church in the morning. You going to be there too?" I asked him.

Kenny nodded. "Sorry about running out of gas today."

"It's okay. I figure our bad guy decided to wait for dark. Maybe after he's read my note, he'll show himself tomorrow." The adrenaline buzz I'd had earlier in the day had been smothered by too many marshmallows. I yawned and hauled myself to my feet.

Iz jumped up too. "I'll walk you home."

Kenny looked over at her in surprise. Then he looked at the short distance separating Gram's house from his. Finally he turned and gave me one of those looks that tells you somebody is trying to work something out in his head.

I had the thought that maybe people didn't give old Kenny nearly enough credit for brain power, because I saw the light bulb go on almost right away. He winked at me and said, "Good idea. Wouldn't want you to get lost, bro. See you tomorrow." And he loped up the slope to his front door.

Whoa—I owed him bigtime for leaving us alone without any flak. Not that I was stupid enough to think he was really going to let it die there, but I'd take whatever harassment I had coming from him without a whimper in the morning.

It really wasn't more than twenty-five feet between the fire ring and the door to Gram's place. I walked as slowly as I could manage, since I suddenly had a lot of big thinking to do. Part of me was thinking how grateful I was that the loon was quiet tonight. Part of me was thinking that I'd have to check for the new tattoo that I apparently had plastered across my forehead, which must have said something like "I ♥ Iz," since it seemed as if everybody was clued into this little thing we had going, despite the fact that I wasn't completely sure what was up with it myself.

But most of me was thinking about how exactly you got the kissing thing started and what exactly you were supposed to do with your noses and where exactly it was safe to put your hands.

We had reached Gram's house, and I guess I was just staring off into space, looking like an idiot with all that overthinking, because Iz finally said, "Trav?" with this big question mark at the end, sounding confused but kind of hopeful, too.

This was it! I tipped toward her, closer and closer,

watching her eyelashes fan against her cheeks as she closed her eyes.

Then Jen's voice floated out the window again. "Iz! Now!"

Iz's eyes popped open. She sighed and turned toward Kenny's house. Then she quickly leaned back toward me and gave me a soft kiss on the cheek, running off before I could do more than blink.

I stood there alone, listening to the breeze gossiping its way through the trees, whispering about the two of us like the newest rumor working its way down the school hallways at lunchtime. Then I ran my fingers down the cheek she had kissed and squeezed my fist, tightly. If only I could catch hold of the kiss, maybe I could hang on to the feel of those soft lips despite everything else that was going on.

I glanced at the lake as I turned to go inside. And saw a boat's running lights gliding across the dark, headed straight toward the darker bulk of the island.

CHAPTER 20

I admit, I have a lot of questions about the Big Guy in the Sky. But Gram had made it clear that as far as she was concerned, He had game, man. So when the two of us settled into a church pew the next morning, I tried, for Gram's sake, to grab on to some holy.

Plus, I was thinking that if the worst happened and the note writer came gunning for me, it might help to have the Big Guy on my side.

Problem was, on that particular Sunday I was too distracted to make time for The Man Upstairs. I was too busy trying to figure out that other man in my life, the bank-robbing one, and all the problems kicking up around him.

Not to mention that I got extra distracted once I

recognized the back of Iz's head just six pews in front of us.

But I was sitting next to my grandmother in a church, so I really worked to push any thoughts of Iz aside. As soon as I cleared out a little space in my brain, this other thought popped through, and I started obsessing about the Monopoly money and the note we'd buried on the island and wondering whose boat I'd seen traveling out there in the dark.

I checked out the other heads in church—well, the backs of them, anyway—and wondered which one of them was trying to catch me while I was trying to catch him. When would he make his next move? And what would it be?

Was I going to need a miracle to stay in one piece?

Then Iz turned and looked over her shoulder all casually, like she was just scanning the room, but as soon as her eyes lit on me, they stayed stuck and she gave me that secret smile, and next thing I knew, Gram was having to poke me in the shoulder because everybody else was standing up to sing and I was just sitting there, all caught up in thinking about Iz.

Then the service was finally over, but rather than making the speedy exit I had planned, I got trapped by

Gram's peeps, who were circling like turkey vultures to pluck up the backstory about my winning chicken-crap ticket.

I finally escaped the posse and headed outside. I was kind of hiding out in a little nook, trying to spot Iz, when some lady who looked like a walking flower garden planted herself in front of me.

"Travis, right?" She had one of those smiles where you could see way too many teeth. "My, you do look like your father, don't you? But I suppose the real question is, are you like him both inside and out?"

I thought I had perfected my delivery-to-the-following-recipient-failed-permanently look. But Mrs. Flower Garden must have misinterpreted my blank stare, because she just kept plowing on.

"Of course, none of us knew exactly how much trouble your father had in him until it was too late, did we?"

She was giving me the same look that the wolf had given Little Red Riding Hood. Just as I was opening my mouth to comment on what big teeth she had, a hand slipped into mine.

"Hello, Mrs. Svengrud," said Iz.

Another Svengrud? What was with this family?

Why did they hate me so much? Maybe one of them *had* written the anonymous note, even if it wasn't Cody. At the very least I was sure they were the reason the whole town had turned me into their fall guy.

Maybe they had actually found the stupid money long ago and now they were the ones spending it; Iz had said King Svengrud had been searching hard for it. Had he somehow pretended to find the bait money the day I'd been in his store so he could frame me for having the cash and then finally spend it himself?

The Teeth turned on Iz and then her eyes dropped down to check out our PDA. "Isabella, you poor dear, how are you feeling after all that trouble with your father the other night?"

I felt Iz's hand jerk in mine, but then she gave me a squeeze that clearly meant "be quiet." "Oh, how nice of you to be thinking about me when you have your own worries. Kenny told me Cody is having big trouble in summer school. Poor thing—did he have to stay home and study? Is that why he isn't at church this morning? I can't imagine how hard it will be on all of you if he flunks again and can't play football in the fall."

I was so happy to see the return of the evil fairy that I couldn't completely hold back a smirk.

Queen Svengrud heaved a big breath that set all her flowers waving in the breeze. She stared at Iz for a moment, but then she seemed to figure out there was no way she could make her fighting weight class and she turned back to me.

"I just worry for your poor grandmother, don't you? After all those years of coping with your father's wild ways, she really deserves to just relax, doesn't she? But now . . ."

"There's Trav's grandma now. Mrs. Stoiska, here he is." Iz raised her voice and yanked me away before I could say, "Bite me," or rearrange the barracuda's teeth to match Linnea's.

Gram didn't seem to be anywhere in sight but I wasn't about to argue. We pulled up next to Kenny.

"I saw boat lights heading out for the island last night, right before I went to bed," I said as soon as it was just the three of us.

"Whoa—so today really could be D-day." Kenny stuffed a whole doughnut into his mouth. I checked out the other two he was still holding, wondering how I could snatch one away without his noticing.

He must have sensed I was posing a threat to his food supply, because he pulled back a step. Then he started giving me this look that was a cross between the evil eye and a smirk. I followed his eyes down and realized he had picked up on my whole hand-holding thing with Iz. Man, it was starting to seem like I was setting myself up for even more crap from Kenny than from the note writer.

And while I was busy turning red, he shoved both remaining doughnuts into his mouth at once.

"Kenny!" We looked over and saw Big Ken pointing at his watch. Kenny swallowed the last of the doughnuts and looked from me to Iz. "I gotta go get in the lineup. You two coming to the parade?" he asked.

Earlier that morning Gram had said something about a Fourth of July parade, but I hadn't paid much attention.

"You'll watch with me, right?" Iz asked eagerly. "Everybody else in the family is in it. Even Linnea is marching with the baton twirlers. Let's go down and be there for the start of the route."

A gang of Linneas armed with batons sounded like a whole new level of scary, but for the chance to spend the afternoon alone with Iz—well, with Iz and a parade route full of people—it was worth the risk. And I needed to make myself publicly available so the note writer could find me, right?

"Yeah," I said. "Just let me find Gram and tell her."

Gram said she and her posse liked to watch from right there in the churchyard. I agreed to stop back for her after the last float had floated by.

"I'm starving," I said as Iz and I headed toward the other end of town. "I guess I didn't pay enough attention when Gram told me lunch would be late today."

"The Frosty Freeze is open," Iz said. "They always make a killing on parade day."

We waited our turn for ice cream. It was clearer than ever that in Boondocks I was some kind of D-list celebrity; people were slapping their eyes on us from all the way down the street at the Big Store. I remembered Iz's fight with Kenny; it probably wasn't doing her reputation as a freak any good to be seen playing guide dog for the outlaw's spawn, but she looked happier than she'd been all week, so I gave up worrying and bought her a double cone.

We wandered farther down the road, searching

for an open spot on the curb so we could sit. Iz spotted a space right in front of the giant fish statue and we settled in.

I looked over my shoulder. "That's got to be the ugliest fish I've ever seen. What kind is it, anyway?"

"Bullhead," said Iz. "Uncle Ken says there aren't even that many of them in the lake. But I think all the other Minnesota fish had already been taken by other towns, so I guess we ended up with the ugly one."

She said it like there was some law that you had to build a giant fish statue to qualify as a Minnesota town. Maybe there was—who knows?

Suddenly I noticed that a shadow had fallen over us. I turned back around and saw Crazy Carl standing there staring, not two feet away.

"It's you again," he said, drilling into me with his watery eyes. "It's you."

Iz pressed her shoulder into mine. "Hey, Carl. How are you?" But it was like she wasn't even there.

Dude was still lasering me with crazy, but then I swear his eyes shifted and somebody inside his head who must have been as sane as anything peeked out at me and said, "I know where it is. I know what you're looking for. And I know where it is."

I could feel my muscles knotting, getting ready to jump up, and Iz must have felt them too, because she put her hand onto my knee to stop me. And in just that space of time, Carl's eyes shifted back to loco again and the Non-Crazy Carl inside his head went back into hiding.

"You stinking space men. Falling into the lake like shooting stars. I'll get you, though."

A siren screamed and I jumped and looked around. The parade was starting; Deputy Dude was cruising by slowly in his sheriff's car to clear the street. Passersby started racing for seats, scrambling in every direction like kids in school hallways when the final bell has rung, and before I could pull it together, Mr. Maniac and his alternate personality had vanished into the crowd.

"Did you *hear* that? I think he knows where the money is!" I was on my feet now, trying to see where Carl had been swallowed up by the river of people.

Iz yanked on the bottom of my shorts and pulled me back down beside her. Her eyes looked even bigger than usual. "Trav, he's always saying strange things. It probably doesn't mean anything."

"No, listen. Gram told me that he used to be really

close to my dad. He totally could know something! I think I should go after him."

"You'll never find him again with all these people around. And I promised Linnea I wouldn't miss the twirlers. Look, I'll help you track him down tomorrow, okay? Cross my heart—we'll spend the whole day looking for him. He lives out at the dump. I'll even take you there if I have to."

She was pretty-pleasing me bigtime with those eyes, so I gave in. Besides, I could tell she was right. The only way I was going to make my way through that crowd was if I got up and marched in the parade itself. And there was no way I was giving anyone another excuse to stare at me.

"I thought this was a small town," I said. "Where'd all these people come from, anyway?"

"All the other small towns around here. And the farm families. Plus, lots of summer people come from The Cities for the holiday weekend. Look, there are the flags!" Iz and everybody around us jumped to their feet; she pulled me up too. When the flags had passed, we all sat down again. So far this parade was a lot like church, what with all the popping up and down.

"Oh, here come the dogs!"

Instead of looking where she was pointing, I turned my head to study Iz. She had that same look on her face that Linnea had the day before: pure, new-bike excitement. Maybe the parade was another one of those things she still loved from when she was a kid.

"There's Jen with the butter head!"

I turned back to the parade to see Big Ken driving a classic convertible with a banner along the side reading PRINCESS KAY OF THE MILKY WAY. Jen, Krissy, and Kari were sitting up on the top of the back seat waving like the Queen of England. They must have changed clothes after church, because they were all rigged up as if it were prom night. The butter head was riding along in the passenger's seat, nestled on a bed of ice. But you could tell the ice wasn't going to be enough to fight off the sun. While I watched, a big, buttery tear slid down poor Butter Head's cheek like she knew she was done for.

I might have felt the same way if it had just been me there at the parade, but it was hard to resist Iz's good time. I even managed not to duck when Linnea threw her baton extra high just for us.

I guess I'd let my guard down by the time the football float drew close.

The flatbed was loaded up with all these beefy jocks carrying buckets of candy to toss out to little kids along the route. Kenny must have been on the other side of the float somewhere; Iz and I still hadn't spotted him when suddenly we were getting bombarded with Tootsie Rolls by Prince Svengrud and a couple of his buddies, thrown hard enough to do damage.

That was it; I'd had about all I was going to take from that family, and I was definitely done letting that loser Cody harass Iz. I pushed her behind the giant bullhead and started after him. I kept going despite having to duck regular barrages of ammo; I had just about caught up with the float when somebody stepped out of the crowd and swung me around by the arm.

"Going somewhere, young man?" asked King Svengrud. I yanked away just in time to crash into the high school band. They had marched up without my noticing, and next thing I knew, I was getting elbowed by some chick with a triangle, making me bounce off the bass drum. I was finally taken down altogether by the tuba dude, ending up at the mercy of the high-heeled boots of the pompom girls. They stepped around me without breaking stride, stomping along to that "Yankee Doodle Dandy" song.

I hid my head until the pompoms were past and then debated just staying where I was in the hopes of being flattened by some giant horses that were clomping by. Or maybe the pooper-scooper guys running along behind them would shovel me up into the manure wagon. But Iz scurried over and grabbed my hand to haul me up and over to the safety of the curb.

"Are you okay?" she asked. She had this weird look on her face, and I didn't even try to guess what she was thinking. There was no way around it—you'd have to practice for years to blow the knight-on-a-white-horse routine any worse than I had.

"Wait until you see my encore. It's a killer," I muttered. I dropped her hand and leaned over to dust off my knees, when Iz made this odd sound. When I straightened up, she was holding her hand over her mouth, trying to push back a laugh.

"I'm sorry," she gasped on the back end of a snort. "I know it's probably not funny to you."

I decided there was no point in pretending I had any dignity left. Especially when most of the crowd was still staring at me instead of the parade. So I gave in and slid Iz a little grin. "Guess you had to be there, huh?"

She stopped laughing and leaned her shoulder into me. "I can't believe that idiot Cody Svengrud. No wonder you hate this town."

"Yeah, well, there are some things here I like pretty good." I reached for her hand again and looked around. "Looks like we missed the end of the parade. Everybody seems to be packing it in."

People were folding up chairs and dragging along screaming munchkins, drifting out into the street to form a tail to the parade.

One old guy gave me a pat on the back as he walked by. "Thought you were roadkill there for sure, boy."

We jostled along with the crowd. I guess the band had only two songs in their rotation; every time they started up on the "Yankee Doodle" one again, Iz got another fit of the giggles.

We met up with Gram at the church, and Iz headed off to hook up with Kenny's family at the end of the route. Gram and I loaded into the truck, and she set off on this roundabout way home to avoid the roadblocks.

"What happened with the football float?" asked Gram.

"Whaddya mean?" Had news of my roadkill act really made it down the street faster than I had?

"Something must have happened," said Gram. "I thought maybe you'd seen it. By the time the float reached the church, there was this huge fight going on. Kenny and the Svengrud boy seemed to be in the middle of it all. Pastor Jackie's husband had to run out and break things up. I'm afraid Cody's nose might never be the same again."

I couldn't help but let loose a laugh. Gram gave me a suspicious look.

"Okay," I said. "I know you're going to say that violence is never the answer and all that crap that adults have to say. But sometimes guys just have to handle things, you know?"

Gram gave me another look. "And what exactly was Kenny handling today?"

"That stupid Svengrud kid thought it was a good joke to pelt me and Iz with candy," I said. "Kenny must have been telling him to lay off. I was going to do it, but old man Svengrud stopped me. What is with that family? They hated me on sight."

Gram sighed. "It's probably . . . Your father and Cody's father were always big rivals. They went head-to-head for everything from football captain to home-coming king to girlfriends. I know it seems silly, but sometimes these things carry over to the next generation in a small town."

"So that's why they hate *me*," I said. "But what's the stupid kid got against Iz?"

This time Gram smiled. "I'm only guessing, Travis, but Cody's family has a lot of money, and he's something of a football star—those things make him a big fish in a small pond around here. And those aren't the kind of things that impress Isabella the way they might some girls. Add to that the fact that she can be a rather . . . *direct* young lady, and I can only assume she made her disdain overly obvious when she spurned Cody's advances."

I thumbed through my mental dictionary and finally translated Gram's words. "You mean you think he *likes* her?" I could hear the outrage in my own voice.

Gram laughed outright. "Finally something the two of you agree on." She pulled the truck to a stop in her driveway. "The garbage cans at church were overflowing. I volunteered to bring some trash home to get it out of the way. The bags are in the back. Will you please carry them up to the garbage can for me?"

I hauled the trash as fast as I could, suddenly realizing how hungry I was. But when I charged into the kitchen, I almost barreled over Gram, who was standing just inside the door. I reached out to steady her and then stepped around her.

"Gram, what—"

The words died in my throat. The kitchen was a disaster. Dried noodles were scattered everywhere. Cereal crunched under my feet. The chairs were knocked over. The door to the fridge was wide open. Broken glass littered the countertop.

And a wickedly sharp butcher knife had been used to skewer a small pile of Monopoly money into the wooden kitchen table.

CHAPTER 21

I t's all my fault," I blurted out.

Gram and I were once again sitting at the kitchen table with Deputy Dude. Only this time he'd just gotten back from taking the knife and the Monopoly money out to his sheriff's car.

"You'd better tell us everything, son."

I didn't think they could send you to juvie for being a complete doofus, but I could already feel the handcuffs. Worst thing was, I deserved whatever happened to me for putting that make-it-stop-hurting look into Gram's eyes.

I really wished I'd listened when Iz had told me that answering the anonymous note that way was a stupid move.

I pulled the original note out of my pocket and

unfolded it on the tabletop. "Somebody left this in Gram's truck the night of the church fundraiser. So I wrote him back an answer, kind of hinting that maybe I do know where the bank money is, and I buried it out on the island with the Monopoly money." I waved around at the mess in the kitchen. "This whole thing was a message for me. He came here to look for the real money, and when he didn't find it, he upped the ante in this weird game of chicken we're playing."

While Deputy Dude studied the note, I made myself look at Gram. Since we'd found the place trashed, her face had changed; it looked like the skin was coming loose from her bones.

"I'm really, really sorry, Gram. I was just trying to get him to come out into the open. I wanted to find out what he knew about my dad."

"It's all right. I understand." Gram reached out and put her hand over mine when she spoke, but two things were obvious: it wasn't all right, and she didn't understand.

Deputy Dude broke in before I could say any more to her. "This isn't a game. This guy's made it clear you don't want to mess with him. It's very important that you tell me where you have the money before some-body gets hurt."

"I don't have the money, I swear! I was just pre-tending to have it, to draw this dude out." Even though I could see why I'd lost all my credibility, I felt myself resenting the fact that I was somehow still the bad guy in his eyes.

"Kyle, if he says he doesn't have the money—" started Gram, but the deputy flattened both of his hands out on the table and leaned forward.

"Mrs. Stoiska, we don't have time to mess around anymore. Next time—and I'm pretty sure there will be a next time—the consequences could be much worse."

"Seriously, if I had the money, I'd give it to you." I tried to keep my voice low and steady, but I could hear it cracking a little at the end. "You think I want to take the chance he'll do something even more horrible next time?"

Deputy Dude skewered me with his eyes the way the butcher knife had skewered the Monopoly money. A silence as thick as blood settled around us.

Finally he seemed to make up his mind about some-thing. He gave a little nod and leaned in really close to me. "Son, I really want to help you out here, but you have to tell me whatever you know before it's too late."

The look he was giving me was trying to say, *The policeman is your friend.* But he could put on all the sincere looks he wanted—it was still coming through loud and clear that in his eyes I was guilty until proved innocent.

I couldn't give him money I didn't have. All I had were wild suspicions, nothing more solid than the evidence he had against me. Even if I did start accusing other people to save my own butt, I could just predict the look the deputy would get in his eyes if I told him about any of *my* suspects.

Like the crazy old man who jabbered about aliens any chance he got. Or the Svengrud family. So what if Cody hadn't been in church that morning and would have had time to trash Gram's house? It wasn't like Deputy Dude was going to go over and start accusing the town royalty on the say-so of Bank-Robber Boy.

And there was still the possibility that my father might be out there somewhere, not actually dead after all. I was sure my dad's old best friend would have loved to hear my whole zombie-dad theory.

I shook my head.

He shook his head too. Finally he turned to Gram.

"Whoever this was might have taken the chance to grab a few other things when he didn't find the bank money. Was anything missing when you looked around?"

"Only one thing. There used to be a box under my bed. There wasn't anything valuable in it, just some keepsakes about John. But it's gone," Gram said.

I felt my shoulders jerk, and they both turned to look at me.

"Something else you've forgotten to share, son?"

It didn't seem as if the box could possibly have anything to do with the break-in, but the whole I've-got-a-secret thing really wasn't working for me at that point, so I confessed. "I took the box. It's safe under my bed."

Gram moved her hand away from mine.

Deputy Dude stood up real slow and put the anonymous note into a plastic bag. Then he wrote something on a business card and set it onto the table. "That's my cell number. You suddenly think of something important you need to tell me, you call that direct. And you might want to start locking your doors. Safer that way for both of you."

He nodded his head at Gram. "I've got to get back

downtown. Place is a zoo because of the holiday. Be careful. And remember, son, I'm just trying to help you." He walked out, pulling the door shut behind him.

We sat there for a minute, neither one of us saying anything. Then I jumped up and waved my hand toward the door. "I just have to—" I ran outside. Deputy Dude was backing his car out of the driveway, but he must have seen me heading his way, because the car jerked to a stop.

His driver's window slid down as I ran up. "You think of something you wanted to tell me away from your grandma?"

I gripped the edges of his car door and leaned closer to the open window. I could hear my words falling over themselves as I tried to get everything out at once. "I know I can't make you believe I don't have the money. But you said you wanted to help me. Whether I have the money or not, it's still your job to catch whoever did this to Gram. You knew my dad—who do you think helped him rob that bank? What really happened that summer? Maybe if we can figure that stuff out, we can figure out who did this, too."

The deputy sighed and looked away. I watched his

fingers drum the top of the steering wheel. Then he looked back at me.

"I can't give you the answers to those questions, kid. I did think of him as my friend. But turns out in the end we weren't real friends after all. There were things he never told me. I didn't really know him the way I thought I did." Deputy Dude actually looked pretty beat-up when he said that. I thought about what it would be like if, out of nowhere, I heard that Kalooky had done something as stupid as robbing a bank. Would I feel as if I'd never really known him?

The deputy continued. "As far as the money goes, here's the thing. In law enforcement, you learn that lots of times the obvious answer is the right answer. And I'm not real big on coincidences. I mean, sure, I'd like to give you the benefit of the doubt, but the truth is, you and the cash turned up the exact same week. It's almost guaranteed the money's reappearance is connected to you. I'm not saying you meant to do anything wrong. Probably you just stumbled across the cash and didn't know what to do. You were afraid that you'd get into trouble. Or you felt like it was the least your old man owed you. Or you just needed a little spending money. So if there's anything like that you want to tell me, I promise to help you out. I can pull a few strings for the sake of your grandma; you won't be in trouble."

I pressed my lips shut and stared back at him. It was clear the two of us were never going to get anywhere; he was never going to move past the idea that I had the money, that I was just as ready to hide my crimes as my father had been.

Suddenly his radio crackled and a voice said something I couldn't understand. But Deputy Dude nodded at my hands holding down his window. "Sorry. Gotta follow up on this. Like I said, town is a zoo today. But let's talk again real soon, okay?"

He rolled the window back up and accelerated out of the driveway.

I walked slowly back into Gram's house. She was sweeping the kitchen floor; the broom stopped midsweep when I walked in. My eyes locked on the huge slash the butcher knife had made in the tabletop. How many different ways, I wondered, could I find to say sorry to her? I'd thought that invisible wall between us had melted away, but it seemed to be back again, even thicker than when we had started.

"*Do* you have the money?" she suddenly said.

I was so thrown by her question that I blurted out

the first thing that came into my head. "No. Do you?"

Gram gave a little bark of laughter, the kind that was more from surprise than because something was actually funny. Then she squeezed her eyes closed real tight. When she opened them again, she looked at me dead on.

"Travis, I promise you—I don't know anything about the bank money. I would never touch it if I did. It's . . . evil. Think of all the damage it's done to my family, what a very high price tag it's had. It cost me my boy. And because of it, I've had to spend the past fourteen years trying to figure out where I went wrong as a mother. Wondering if my son drowned by accident while he was covering up his crime, or if he decided in the end he couldn't live with what he'd done."

She stopped and looked over at the wall; I finally realized she was staring at the fish key holder my father had made.

She took a deep breath and kept going. "And now it's obvious that the evil of that money has bled into another generation. Look at how it's come between the two of us."

"I never really believed you had the money. It was more—"

"No, it's not about that. Really, putting me on the suspect list was actually logical of you. I'm upset because you didn't come to me with your questions. You snooped around the house and took that box from under my bed without talking to me about it. But I can't really blame you. A lot of this is my fault. I let my being upset over the way your father's life ended turn his whole existence into a secret. I was too ashamed to share him with anyone—even you. I apologize, Travis. You deserve better from me."

I had that ice-cream-headache feeling behind my eyes, and I was pretty sure I was going to start bawling any second. But if I did, Gram would probably see it as proof that she really had let me down. I desperately tried to think of what I could say that would show her it was okay, that I didn't want her to blame herself. It was enough that I blamed myself.

We both jumped when somebody knocked at the door. Gram peered through the window and then turned to me. "It's for you. I'm going to go put on my work clothes so I can keep cleaning up."

I took a deep breath and waited until I was pretty sure I had myself under control. When I finally opened the door, Iz was standing there with a worried look on her face.

"Why was the deputy here again?"

I gestured her inside, and her mouth fell open when she saw the kitchen. She looked back at me.

"You were right," I said. "I was stupid. Somebody didn't like my note. He left the Monopoly money stuck to the table with a big knife as a way of telling me so. And he wrecked Gram's house to prove he means business." My voice sounded wobbly; Mr. Cool had definitely left the building.

Iz didn't say anything—she just walked over and gave me this big hug. Like I said, I had pretty much given up on hugging. I'd forgotten how good it could feel, and of course this one was that much better because it was Iz.

After a while she pulled back. "I came over to see if you could come along to Kenny's grandma's house for the Fourth of July barbeque. But . . ." She looked around doubtfully at the mess in the kitchen.

"Yeah, I need to stay here and help Gram clean up." We were both keeping our voices low.

"I could stay and help too. I don't mind. It won't be as much fun without you, anyway."

It was tempting, but . . . "No thanks. I really think Gram and I need to talk on our own about some stuff."

Iz nodded. "But tomorrow we're on for that trip to the dump, right?"

I guess I looked as blank as I felt because she added, "You know, to track down Carl. So you can figure out if he really does know anything."

I had completely forgotten about going to find Crazy Carl. "Definitely. Now it's more important than ever that I talk to him again. But you really think we'll have to go to the dump?"

Iz shrugged. "Carl turns up in all sorts of crazy places; it's a town joke that you can't keep anything a secret because he's likely to pop up at any time. But the dump is kind of his home now, I guess. I think he goes through the junk as it comes in and sells what he can." She dropped her voice even lower. "Aunt Jen is pretty convinced that your grandma pays Mr. Murphy rent every month so Carl can sleep in that old trailer they use as the dump office. Mr. Murphy pretends that Carl is his official 'security force,' but you know that's not really true."

Even all these years later, was Gram carrying on

where my father had left off, helping to take care of Carl?

Now that Iz had mentioned Carl, I was remembering some of the other details from the parade. "Did Kenny really beat up Cody Svengrud?"

"I think Kenny broke Cody's nose. Kenny's in *so* much trouble." Just for a second this huge smile took over Iz's face, and then she put it away. I wasn't completely clear if she was happy over the broken nose or the thought of Kenny in the doghouse. Maybe both.

"I better go. We won't get home until late because Kenny says his uncle Butch is bringing a bunch of his own fireworks to set off after the official ones are over. But I'll call you on your cell. Have it turned down low so it doesn't wake your grandma, okay? We can figure out what time you want to head out in the morning or maybe even meet down on the dock tonight and . . . say good night."

At least I had one thing to look forward to.

After I closed the door behind Iz, I started tackling the mess in the kitchen, thinking the whole time about what I needed to say to Gram. It was obvious the two of us had a lot of clearing up to do.

CHAPTER 22

Was he really off-the-charts wild?" I asked. Gram and I were working our way through each room, cleaning as we went. It was clear she'd made a decision to tell me the whole truth about my dad; I definitely wasn't getting the children's-chewable version of his story, and some of it was a pretty big pill to gulp down. But I think it helped that we had something else to do with our hands and our eyes; we were both still on a learning curve as far as communicating with one another.

Gram sighed. "I know a lot of people thought of him that way. To me it seemed more like . . . some kind of hunger in him I could never fully feed. From the time he was a tiny boy he charged after life; he was never satisfied waiting for it to come to him."

"Which probably means robbing a bank wasn't the first stupid thing he did."

"No." Gram finished picking up pieces of glass from a broken mirror in her bedroom. "When he was seven, he took the boat out by himself and nearly drowned. When he was fifteen, he was suspended from school for a dangerous prank. The army kicked him out, eventually, although he wouldn't talk to me about that. And in the months before the bank robbery, he made a lot of bad choices. Your mother left after he was arrested for reckless driving."

"So he gave everybody a hard time his whole life." I could hear a note of anger in my voice. "And then he did this final rotten thing and disappeared and left you to answer for him when the FBI showed up."

Gram turned away from folding clothes and looked at me. "Yes. He made some terrible choices. But I made mistakes too, as his mother. To be able to forgive myself, I first had to forgive him."

She stopped talking for a moment and stood staring at a large gash in her mattress.

"I'll flip it over," I said. "I think that way you can still sleep on it for now."

It was a bit of a struggle, but I got it turned over and Gram kept talking.

"But, Travis, your father had some wonderful qualities too. He could be warm and loving and *fun;* no one could stay somber with John in the room."

She pulled out a set of sheets and we started making up the bed. "I don't know if you're old enough to understand how seldom a person is purely good or bad. For instance, I've always believed that the reason John broke into that bank at night was because there was still enough good in him that he couldn't stomach doing it during the day when someone might get hurt. But maybe that's an old woman's way of comforting herself . . ."

Her voice trailed off and she looked out the window at the lake for a moment. "People are like daytime and nighttime, rotating around the clock—at different times a person's light can turn into his greatest darkness. Your father was full of fearlessness, and zest, and had an amazing ability to live fully in the moment. But he never learned to channel the qualities that could have become his greatest assets—instead they turned into impatience, and recklessness, and thoughtlessness about how his actions were going to affect the people around him."

"But you always stuck by him."

"Yes, I was usually there afterward to hear his confession and help him clean up the mess. Now I think it might have done him more good if I hadn't been. But I'll never know the answer to that."

She stuffed a ripped-up pillow into a garbage bag. "There's no halfway about love, Travis. When you love people, you give them the power to hurt you. And there are times they will. I want you to remember something important: it's not a betrayal of love to make it clear to someone that you've reached your limit—that you can't accept any more hurtful behavior."

I turned away and picked up a pile of clothes off the floor of her closet. "So I guess that's what Ma did, right? She reached her limit, so she left?"

"I can't speak for your mother, Travis. But yes, I believe that when she knew you were coming along and she really understood where things were headed for John, she did what she thought was best. I've always respected her for that."

"But maybe if she'd stayed, he would have finally settled down. People do, when they become parents, right? Maybe if she hadn't taken off, it all would have worked out differently. I would have actually gotten to know him."

"Maybe. But you can't blame your mother for trying to protect the two of you. It wasn't her choices that kept you from meeting your father; it was his."

"So Ma left and he figured he might as well rob a bank as the next step up the thrill ladder? No point in trying to become a better person just because he had a kid on the way." That wobble from earlier had come back into my voice; it wasn't turning out to be my most macho day.

Gram stopped straightening the curtains and walked over to put her hands on my shoulders. "Travis, I hope it's not a mistake for me to tell you this —and I might be wrong—but I believe your father robbed that bank because he *did* want a life with you. Stealing that money was idiotic and reckless and it cost him everything, but I think he foolishly let himself believe that if he showed up in California with a way to support a family, he could somehow convince your mother to take him back and let him truly be your father. He made the biggest mistake of his life for the best possible reason."

I pulled away from her and sat down on the freshly made-up bed, checking to see where her trash can was in case I ended up hurling. I think my system was going into honesty overload.

"Which doesn't make it your fault!" said Gram sharply.

I took a deep breath and tried not to choke on it. "So you don't think . . . that he maybe isn't really dead? That he took the stolen money and headed off to Rio or someplace with it because he never really cared about me? And now he's back, and that's why some of the money has turned up?"

Gram didn't say anything for a long time. I couldn't even look at her; instead I watched this huge fly crawl around on her dresser. Its wings buzzed frantically as it kept trying to zero in on the source of the thick dead-flowers smell that hung heavily in the hot air, but we'd done too good a job with our cleanup of the broken perfume bottle.

"No. I told you I made a lot of mistakes as a mother. I might not have managed him well, but I didn't fail to understand who my son was; I recognized his flaws all too painfully. And deliberate cruelty wasn't one of them. I've always known how much your father loved me; he would have never let me go on thinking he was dead if he was alive. You've got to learn to accept that he's gone. I have."

I felt my shoulders slump. Much as there was that part of me that was ticked at the thought that my father could have ignored me all those years, I guess I wanted to keep believing he was going to turn up somehow with a football in his hand, ready for a game of catch.

But Gram wasn't leaving any room for maybe.

She sat down on the bed next to me and put her arm around my shoulders. "I know how hard it must be for you to hear these things. And I'm afraid I need to tell you something you're going to like even less."

She must have felt the way my shoulders tightened up under her arm because she clamped down harder. "I've been trying to think of how to tell you this in a way that you'll understand, but I can't put it off any longer. While you were outside talking to the deputy, I called your mother to let her know what's going on. She's very worried. We ended the call quickly so she could make arrangements for you to fly home in the morning, but she'll be calling back with the details tonight."

"No!" I didn't know what bad news I had been expecting, but it wasn't that. I leaped to my feet, away from her Benedict Arnold arm. "Gram, I know you're mad because this was all my fault, and I've been sneaking around behind your back and stuff, but please don't send me away!"

"Travis, I'm not sending you away. This isn't a punishment. Your mother—"

I didn't let her finish. "She always thinks she knows what's best for me, but she never understands what I really need. I need to be here! Why did you have to call her?"

Gram sighed. "She's your mother. You're thirteen. For now, she has the right to decide what's best for you. At a minimum she had the right to know that you may not be safe here. Like Deputy Anderson said, this isn't a game." She waved her hand at the trash bags full of her ruined things.

"No, Gram, please listen. So far nobody's gotten hurt. I bet Deputy Anderson can figure out who broke in here and arrest him and everything will be fine in a day or two. Please let me stay."

"Travis, I'm sorry. Having you here has brought me incredible joy. But anyone capable of this kind of destruction could be dangerous. I didn't keep my own boy safe. I can't take that chance away from another mother. Your mother has always been generous to me. She was under no obligation to let me be a part of your life, but she has. Please understand that I need to respect her decision in this."

She held out her hand to me, but I backed away from it and she finally dropped it down to her side. "When all of this is cleared up, I'll have you back, I promise. Try to understand."

I kept shaking my head from side to side. "You don't understand what it's like. I hate Ma's new life. There's no place for me anymore." I knew I was being total Drama Dude, but I couldn't help it. I could hear the sound of the front door to my stepfather's house slamming shut and locking me inside, and I knew that this time, there'd be no escape.

No more getting to know Gram through her long silences more than through anything she said. No last chance to quit blowing it and actually kiss Iz. No chance to figure out who this new me—the me who was starting to think he belonged somewhere after all—really was.

She stared directly into my eyes. "I promise that

you will always have a place here. Once it's safe, I'll make your mother understand how important it is to you—to both of us—that you visit again soon. Travis, I love you. This time you need to trust me."

But I just kept shaking my head. Maybe it was my fault for writing that stupid note. Maybe it was my father's fault for robbing that stupid bank. But in that exact moment it all felt like Gram's fault. She had decided to use her powers for evil instead of for good, and as far as I knew, once grownups went over to the dark side, they could never come back again.

CHAPTER 23

Dead man talking. And talking and talking. Not that it did me any good. No matter what I said to Ma, I was still headed straight for the chair, AKA the plane seat that would take me back to California.

"You'll have to leave fairly early tomorrow to get to the airport on time. Your grandmother has already agreed to drive you. They'll have your ticket waiting at the counter." I'd already heard all this ten times; she just kept saying it over all the arguments I came up with.

Suddenly I remembered I had one more weapon left, and I pulled out the big gun. "The deputy said I couldn't leave town. I'm still a suspect."

"Don't be ridiculous, Travis. Your grandmother warned me about that and gave me his cell number.

When I called him and mentioned that my lawyer would be contacting his boss in the morning, he said you were free to leave town immediately."

"Ma, *please*, it's really, really important for me to stay. Please don't make me come back yet."

"Tomorrow. Early. And it's late there now. You'd better go pack your things so you're ready. And if you aren't at LAX when I get there to pick you up, I'm getting straight on a plane and coming out there to drag you home myself. I think we both know how unhappy that would make me."

Yeah, we both knew.

We were quiet for a long moment and then she said, softer, "Trav, I miss you. Don't you think it's time to come home?"

I pulled out the meanest voice I could manage. "You know that's not *my* home."

She sighed, bigtime wind coming at me even through the phone line. Then she said the six most heinous words in the English language: "This is for your own good."

That was the new Ma for you—I try to tell her something is really important to me, and she reduces it to the equivalent of making me eat my vegetables. She kept talking but I hit the end button. Starting tomorrow, it looked as if I had no choice but to spend the rest of my life arguing with her. No reason to spoil the fun by getting an early start.

Gram and I had done what we could to finish cleaning up. I admit, I'd been tempted to lock myself away in my room and leave the traitor to deal with the rest of the chaos herself, but I knew that wouldn't have been right. Maybe I took after my father in that I sometimes made stupid choices, but I wasn't going to be the kind of dude who walked away afterward and made somebody else handle the aftermath.

I was cleaning my bedroom—or really, my ghost father's bedroom, by myself. Gram had made it obvious she wanted to talk some more, but I just couldn't. The entire rest of my life stretched out in front of me, and I wasn't ready to take it like a man.

I hadn't bothered to tell Ma that there really wasn't any need for me to pack; the note writer had pretty much destroyed everything of mine in the room. Wherever I went next—and I wasn't sure yet if it would be back to California or to a galaxy far, far away—I'd be traveling light: the clothes on my back, the cell phone in my pocket, and the Father Box. For some reason the note writer had left it untouched, and I was taking it with me whether Gram liked it or not.

The only thing I'd have to take with me from Iz was that memory I had folded into my hand after she'd kissed my cheek.

But she was going to call me after they got home late so we could say good night. I caught my breath. And so we could figure out when we were going to head out to find Crazy Carl.

Crazy Carl. Who just might know something about the money. The guy that Iz had said knew all the town's secrets.

I mean, okay, the guy was clearly wacko. But there'd been that one minute there when, I swear, he knew what he was talking about. And that was when he'd said that he knew what I was looking for, that he knew where it was.

What if he really did know where the money was? I thought about the card that Deputy Dude had left behind, the one with his cell phone number. I probably should have said something about Carl to him earlier. It wasn't too late to call him now, but then we'd have to have another six-hour conversation about why he still thought I was the one with the money, and we'd never get around to Carl. If I could just find the money myself and turn it over to Deputy Dude, this whole thing would be over. No more reason for the note writer to keep after me, no more danger. No need for me to have to leave tomorrow. And Carl was old, and ready-to-fall-down sick, and Gram had said harmless. No reason I couldn't handle finding out what he knew on my own.

It was the longest of total long shots, but without it I was left high and dry. Good thing Gram was one of those early-to-bed people. I tuned my ears up to bat frequency, waiting to hear the sounds of her settling in for the night. That way I'd know when it was safe for me to sneak out.

And I almost jumped through the ceiling when this huge series of booms exploded outside my window. It sounded like a sail-by shooting.

I'd forgotten about Fourth of July fireworks. It was clear Gram wasn't going to sleep until they were over.

I had plenty of time to sit there and maybe change my mind.

At first I was tempted to just wait until Iz and Kenny got home, to see if they'd go with me. But it seemed like there were a lot of holes in that plan. Iz had said they would be late, and I didn't have any time to waste. What if Crazy Carl wasn't at the dump? What if I had to chase all over the countryside looking for him? I couldn't afford to wait any longer than necessary to get started. Besides, Iz had said Kenny was already in line to be sentenced to some hard time; if he got caught sneaking out, it wouldn't help his case any. My decisions had already ruined Gram's day; no reason I needed to bring more trouble on anybody else's head.

It was probably better if I just handled it on my own. If this whole Crazy Carl thing turned out to be a dead end, nobody even had to know I'd gone to see him. But the longer I sat there and thought about it, the more sense it made that it wouldn't be a dead end.

Why hadn't it occurred to me before that I'd seen Crazy Carl all over town the day King Svengrud had found the bait money? I'd even seen him slapping down a bankroll of bills at the Big Store. Sure, Gram had given him some money at the dump, but I didn't think it had been that much. All the townspeople had been so quick to decide I had the bank cash that they hadn't bothered to remember who else was in the stores spending money that morning.

But if Crazy Carl knew how to get his hands on all that green, why had he waited until now to spend it?

Maybe if he was the accomplice—and I still wasn't sure if I believed that—he had wanted to put some time between the bank break-in and when he started spreading the money around. The FBI had handed out those bait-money lists to all the local stores. Maybe Carl had known about that and had wanted to hang low for a while. And then he went crazy and kind of forgot how the whole money thing worked and didn't even understand he was sitting on enough stolen pesos to buy the dump for himself if he wanted to.

Or maybe he *hadn't* waited until I'd turned up in town to start spending it. Maybe he'd been spending the money all these years, a little at a time, but nobody had ever bothered to check the bait-money list until I'd showed up to play Pin the Crime on the New Kid.

Or like I said, maybe he wasn't the accomplice at all; he was just a guy who'd stumbled across somebody else's high-priced secret.

I thought I was going to go crazy myself, having to sit there and wait to find out what Carl knew.

Then there was this one last giant boom, and

everything quieted down. I waited a while longer until I was sure it was safe and then creaked my door open, listening until I heard these little popping snorts Gram makes while she's sleeping.

She'd shown me where she kept a big flashlight in the kitchen for when the lights went out in storms and stuff; I didn't remember seeing it broken like most of the dishes from the cupboard, but I kept my fingers crossed anyway. I heaved a sigh of relief when the flashlight clicked on with no problem. Making the trip along that rutted-up road on a bike at night was going to be bad enough, let alone without any kind of light.

Once I got outside, I looked over at Kenny's house —totally dark, and no van in the driveway. They weren't home yet.

I set out, thinking through the route Gram had taken when we'd gone to the dump with the garbage from the freezer chest. Holy crap—was it really possible that had been only a few days ago?

I turned the flashlight off when I got to town, not wanting to call any attention to myself just in case anybody was wandering around in a post-fireworks daze. But it was quiet, with no sounds other than a car somewhere off in the distance and a hum coming from the back of the grocery store. Maybe that was where Crazy Carl's aliens parked their spaceship.

The giant bullhead rose up in the dark like some kind of prehistoric monster. It wasn't the night-light dark you get in a real city; the two streetlights splashed only small pools of yellow into the blackness. No help from above, either: it was that dying kind of moon, the sliver-thin scythe carried by the Grim Reaper.

I kept my eyes peeled as best I could in case Crazy Carl was hanging out somewhere in town, but there was no sign of him. I turned down the road I was pretty sure led to the dump, and within a few feet the darkness swallowed me up again. As soon as I clicked my flashlight back on, a pair of red-hot eyes glowed out at me from a ditch. Whoever owned the eyes vanished too fast for me to tell, but I sure hoped it was one of Gram's partying raccoons rather than something with longer fangs.

I pedaled faster. Fortunately the road tunneled straight ahead through the dark, so I could focus all intensely on the road surface itself and avoid the worst of the holes. I was also trying to work out how I was going to get the sane person inside of Crazy Carl's head to come out and talk to me, when suddenly my cell started jingling and I just about steered into the ditch.

Had Gram figured out I'd gone AWOL? Had Ma called back with another set of marching orders? I pulled to a stop, fished my phone out of my pocket, and looked at the screen. It was coming from Kenny's house. How could I have forgotten Iz was going to call me?

I hit answer. "Hey. I guess you're home. Did you have fun at Kenny's grandma's?"

"What's wrong? Your voice sounds funny."

"Uh . . . long story. Listen, I'm not going to be able to meet you tonight." For some reason, I wanted to keep my little joy ride on the DL. Maybe it felt like asking for bad luck to say anything about what I was doing until I made sure I was right about Crazy Carl.

There was a long pause and finally she said, "Okay," but in this kind of voice where I knew right away her feelings were hurt.

"Look," I said hurriedly. Forget luck—I didn't need luck when I had evidence, and the guy clearly knew something. "I really wish I could. But the truth is I'm not there. I'm on my way to the dump to find Carl."

"You're going to the dump tonight? Trav, are you crazy?"

"Yeah, maybe," I said. "But listen—my mom found

out everything and she's ordered me home. First thing tomorrow. For my own good, she said. I've got to get Carl to tell me where the money is. I mean, I've been thinking it all through—he could even be the accomplice, right? And then when that's cleared up, I can talk Ma into letting me stay after all."

I was talking too fast and Iz probably couldn't make sense of half of it, but this little jump of panic kept frogging up in my throat, and I knew I had to get moving again soon or I'd chicken out and turn back, wasting my last chance.

"I can't believe you're going to the dump on your own in the middle of the night to talk to some crazy guy you think might be a bank robber," she said. "Trav, think about what happened today to your grandma's house. Somebody out there is really ticked at you. I think you're being stupid again."

I guess a couple little near kisses weren't powerful enough to make the evil fairy vanish in a poof of smoke.

"Look, this is the only way I can stay in Minnesota. That's what you want too, right?" I said.

"I want you to stay, but mostly I want you not dead," she said. "Boys are always such idiots, with all that macho crap. How could you do this on your own?"

"Look, I'll be fine, really. You're blowing this way out of proportion. I'm pretty sure I'm most of the way there already, and Gram says she's never known Carl to hurt a flea. I'll talk to him real quick and come home, and by morning this will all be worked out, okay? I'll get to stay, and we can just focus on having some fun for a change."

"All I'm saying is that maybe it's not the worst thing in the world that your mom *wants* you home with her," she said.

Even through the phone I could tell that the Ice Age had returned. There was no way I could answer that comment directly without the risk of being turned into a freezer pop, so I said, "Don't worry so much, okay? It's really no big deal."

"Fine. Don't listen to me. It's not like I've been right about anything else." I could hear Iz slam the phone down.

I guess she wasn't buying my "no big deal."

To tell the truth, I wasn't either. Right about then, my whole little midnight ride of Paul Revere was starting to feel like a very big deal. Or maybe like another very big mistake on my part.

But if it was, it was a mistake even Iz couldn't stop me from making.

CHAPTER 24

After Iz hung up on me, I just sat there for a long time, wondering if I had completely blown it with her. Even if everything worked out and I got to stay in Minnesota, was she going to give me anything but the cold shoulder?

And even if I did track down Crazy Carl, who was to say I'd be able to make any sense out of his Looney Tunes alien talk?

And even if he did admit to being the accomplice, what if I still couldn't put my hands on the money? There was no telling if he'd repeat the same story tomorrow morning for anybody else. Who would believe he'd confessed about the bank heist to me? The townsfolk would probably see the whole thing as my pitiful attempt to lay the blame on somebody too crazy to defend himself. *Go pick on somebody your own mental-health status, Bank-Robber Boy!*

But really, I had to be close to the dump. What did I have to lose at that point, other than a little of my life's blood to a random wandering vampire and/or the swarm of mosquitoes trying to suck me dry?

I kicked off on my bike and kept going. It seemed to take forever, but finally I could tell I was almost there; the rotting-zombies smell slithered into my nostrils. When I pulled to a stop at the gate, the smell tried to smother me from the inside. Once I was done dry heaving, I leaned my bike against the fence. The thick air and my own nerves had me sweating like a roomful of *American Idol* wannabes.

The gate was pulled closed with a padlock and chain; just on the off chance they were rusted out, I tested the gate to make sure it was actually locked. The dark shape of the trailer loomed up inside. Was Crazy Carl nestled all snugly in there with his buddies, the cockroaches?

"Hey! Carl. I gotta talk to you. Come on out here and let me in!"

Nothing.

"Carl!" I rattled the gate. Finally I just hauled

myself up and over the chainlink fence and dropped down onto the other side.

I climbed the steps of the trailer and banged on the door. "Yo! Carl."

Something clattered behind me and I whipped around. I couldn't see anyone. I ran the flashlight beam up and down a mound of garbage. It caught the long tails of two scurrying shapes.

Rats! Literally.

But no Crazy Carl.

I tried the trailer door handle and it pushed open under my hand. It was so small inside that I didn't even have to leave the doorway to see everything. I ran my light across a beat-up old desk and file cabinet, a chair with broken slats, and an empty mattress on the floor. A rusted-out toilet sat in a back corner.

There was no sign of the whacked-out possible felon who was my only hope.

I pulled the door shut behind me. I wandered a few feet farther along the road that wound through the dump, straight into the pits of hell. Plastic garbage bags were mounded on all sides. They glinted in the flashlight beam like butcher knives in the hands of psycho killers. I spied something red and wet and glistening. I made myself keep moving.

The misshapen mounds of trash cast creepy shadows ahead of me. I raised the flashlight higher. I was surrounded by mountains of slime. That first day Gram and I had been out here, I'd watched Carl scramble his way over the piles of garbage. He could be anywhere in that wilderness of waste.

I searched among a million or so bags, but finally I stopped. For all I knew, I was circling the same mound over and over. I was never going to find Crazy Carl like this. The question was, should I keep searching there at the dump, or was he somewhere else?

I was debating my options when I heard a car coming down the road. My gut clenched. I didn't think Crazy Carl had wheels, but I also couldn't figure out who else would be visiting the dump at that time of night. I flicked off my light and scurried behind one of the piles.

I heard a car door slam shut.

"Hey! Kid! I know you're here. The bike's a dead giveaway. Get on out here."

It was Deputy Dude. How had he tracked me down? Had Iz turned me in?

I was plenty ticked at the thought, but maybe in the end it would save some time. I'd tell him what Crazy Carl had said at the parade and all the stuff I'd figured out about Carl spending money in town. Then I'd point out that it was his deputy duty to help me nail the bank-robbery accomplice. I should have just called him before.

I could hear his heavy footsteps coming closer; he must have climbed over the fence too. When his flashlight beam was arcing toward my hiding place, I stepped out from behind the mound.

"There you are. So the money's out here somewhere?"

The guy had caught on to the whole Crazy Carl theory pretty fast; maybe that was why they let him carry the big gun.

"I don't know. I mean, maybe, but I haven't been able to ask him yet." I threw an arm up to shield my eyes; the deputy kept shining his light right in my face.

"Look, kid, I don't know what your new game is, but the rules just changed. Now, tell me where you've got the cash."

At first I figured he had missed the part where Carl had taken my spot on the bad-guy roster. But when I opened my mouth to explain, Deputy Dude changed the batting order altogether. "After I got the phone call from your mother, I knew I didn't have any more time to mess around. And since I didn't find the cash when I searched your granny's house, I figured you'd be heading out to pick it up tonight. You get points for thinking of the dump as a hiding place, kid. But now it's time to hand it over. I liberated all that money fourteen years ago, and I want it back now."

It was like he was speaking Swahili, and I didn't know how to translate. He finally decided to help me catch up to the story line. He lowered the flashlight beam out of my eyes so I could see, pulled his gun out of the holster, and pointed it straight at me.

"You're the accomplice?" my voice squeaked out. How could he be the accomplice? Crazy Carl was the one at the stores spending the money. That was why I was there at the dump in the first place.

"I don't know that you'd call me an accomplice when the whole bank heist was my idea from the start. All that energy I spent convincing your father to help me out, and then he didn't even hide the money on the island like we'd agreed. I should have figured he'd start second-guessing it all afterward. Idiot never told me he'd stashed the money somewhere else. Stupid on my part to get rid of him before I discovered that."

I opened my mouth again but this time no sound at all came out. I just did that fish thing, where you keep opening and closing your lips.

"I don't have any more time to waste, kid. You've got exactly ten seconds to tell me where the money is before I shoot you in the kneecap and wherever else it takes for you to tell me what I want to know. Ten. Nine. Eight."

I was sucking in air too fast. My head was spinning.

"Seven. Six. Five."

Somebody let out a scream.

I thought I had to be hallucinating. But the deputy heard it too. He whipped around to see who was behind him. I took off like a rabbit in the other direction.

The screaming continued. I just kept running.

I skidded between two mounds of garbage. I careened around a half-buried refrigerator. In between screams I could hear Deputy Death crashing around behind me. He was hot on my trail.

I dropped my flashlight. I didn't dare use it anyway. I smacked dead-on into something hard. I bounced off and kept going. Something slimy slapped across my face.

I kept moving. I scrambled through spots too tight for Deputy Death. I thought I was losing him.

Then something rolled under my foot. My ankle twisted and I went down hard in a pile of garbage. I hoisted myself back up. But as soon as I tried to put weight on my foot, it gave out under me.

The screaming had stopped. Everything seemed to have slowed down. I could hear the deputy's boots squishing closer.

I looked around. Three steps to my left stood an old freezer chest. The top was missing. A mannequin stood inside.

I crawled over to it. Somehow I hauled myself over the edge. I hunkered into the bottom. Something was clogging my throat. I swallowed and tasted my own blood.

There wasn't enough air in the universe for my busted-out lungs. I hid my face in my knees to muffle my gasps. My ankle was pulsing like a bass note pouring out of a lowrider. Sweat waterfalled off me.

I don't know how long I huddled there just trying to breathe. As soon as I could suck air quietly enough, I lifted my head to listen for Deputy Death. My gamble seemed to have paid off; it sounded as if he had moved past me. I looked skyward. I couldn't see any sign of his flashlight beam.

I fumbled in my pocket. *Yes!* My cell phone was still there. I yanked it out and then stared at it. What good did it do me? No way I could risk calling someone and having the deputy overhear. My cover would be blown as soon as I said anything.

Deputy Death's voice cut through the dark. "Might as well give yourself up, kid. I'll get to you sooner or later, and riling me up is just going to make it more painful for you."

There was nobody I could text. Even with the time difference, Ma would be sound asleep, and Kalooky was off surviving the wilderness.

"Look, kid, we can do this the easy way or the hard way. But I can promise you one thing: the more worked up I am when I find you, the more hurt you'll feel."

It seemed like his voice was coming from a different direction, but I didn't think he was any nearer to me. It was a big dump. I was fine where I was. It didn't even smell that bad anymore. I'd just stay hidden until morning. Once somebody showed up to open for business, I'd be safe.

I wondered what time the vultures showed up.

"Of course, maybe a tough guy like you isn't worried about a little pain. But you've got to remember to think about the big picture, kid. Like your granny, for instance. I mean, I might be willing to swing a little deal with you there." Deputy Death's voice was still loud, but it had shifted to this slick super-salesman tone.

"I guess you're smart enough to have figured out it's too late to save yourself, kid. You're dead meat. But you can still choose to make things easier for poor old Granny. You cooperate with me, and I'll leave her alone."

Suddenly I remembered that among the dozens of apps I had loaded onto my phone was a recorder. I crouched over my cell to hide any light and fumbled with the buttons. My hands were shaking but I managed to get it running. Now he could make all the threats he wanted—the more the better. Then, when I managed to escape, I'd have enough evidence to bust him.

"You keep stretching things out this way, and I'll make sure Granny pays a high price."

I saw a light beam pass high overhead. Was he doubling back?

"Come on, kid. You want the last thing Granny hears to be a description of exactly how I killed her son?"

His voice was definitely closer now. I sank down lower. I tucked my phone into a far corner of the freezer and felt around with my hands to see if there was anything on the floor I could throw at him. Where was Butter Head when I needed her?

"Or maybe it's really worse to let Granny live a nice long life never knowing the truth. When you don't turn up tomorrow, she'll just assume you ran off again. You're good at that, right? When you never come back, she'll box up your stuff and stick it under the bed next to what's left of your old man's life. Both of you gone without her ever knowing where or how."

I think my heart was bleeding. Gram was as good as dead no matter what; I knew she wouldn't survive having somebody else she loved vanish without a trace.

"You come out now and I'll fix it so she doesn't have to go through any of that."

The light beam swung overhead again. Maybe I could heave the mannequin at him? Or jump him when he got closer? I tried putting weight on my injured ankle and almost bit through my lip to keep from screaming.

"Granny's been good to you, right? Give yourself up for her, kid."

I could hear his boots squishing again. Definitely getting closer.

For a desperate couple of seconds I tried to come up with a great lie I could sell him. That was one of my mad skills, right? I could pretend I'd hidden the money somewhere and convince him I had to lead him to it—somewhere buried on the island, maybe? Then I'd find a way to escape on our way out there. Escape and save both me and Gram.

But it was like he was wired for psychic sound or something. "And don't bother thinking up some elaborate escape plan, kid. You're mine."

The voice was louder. He was definitely closing in. My brain was wiped clean of ideas. It looked as if I had been right that very first morning in Minnesota: the ghosts of all those dead animals in Gram's freezer were going to have their revenge on the son of the man who'd hunted them down.

I made myself as invisible as possible.

"I didn't like having to get rid of your old man, you know. But he admitted to me he'd left his backup flashlight in the bank vault. As soon as he said it, I knew they'd track him down. And get him to talk. Your dad was always a big talker. And I couldn't have that. So . . . he really didn't leave me any other choice. And it was easy to send everyone on a wild-goose chase."

I was maybe minutes away from dying in a freezer chest because my father had been a bigmouth. And a screwup. He'd even managed to screw up *while* he was screwing up.

I was a screwup too. I'd pretty much built my own deathtrap. Both Gram and I were going to pay the price. And Ma too, I realized.

"I got a look at the case files myself, once I became a deputy. He'd wiped the outside of the flashlight clean, but he'd never wiped his fingerprints off the batteries."

The footsteps stopped. I could hear the deputy's heavy breathing.

All of a sudden, I could somehow picture myself

cornered like a rat in the appliance of death, like I was seeing it all happen from above. The way people always described near-death experiences.

Ma, I'm sorry. I am so, so sorry.

Then I saw a really bright light.

"Near-death" was exactly the right name for it. Because it was Deputy Death's flashlight shining straight down on me.

"Gotcha," he said.

CHAPTER 25

You make it too easy, kid. Like shooting fish in a barrel." Deputy Death leaned close and pointed his gun at me again. "Now, we'd counted down through five, I think. One last chance to tell me where the bank money is or I shoot you, right? Four . . ."

I started to open my mouth to tell him I'd lead him to the money. Anything to buy time.

"Three."

But somewhere between "three" and "two," something leaped up out of the deepest, darkest part of my brain. And I realized that I *did* know exactly where the money was.

"Two."

"I know where it is! Help me out of here and I'll show you—"

But before I could say any more, there was a thump and the deputy gave this little sigh. First his flashlight dropped into my lap, and then his gun. He started sliding down the outside of the freezer. His jaw whacked hard against the edge, and then his head vanished from my sight.

I didn't have a clue what had just happened. But now I was the one holding a gun.

I still couldn't get my ankle to work, so I sat there with the gun pointed, waiting for Deputy Death's head to pop back up over the edge like one of those punching-bag clowns that you knock over as hard as you can but always bounce right back up.

I've always hated clowns.

But he didn't. Pop back up, I mean. Instead, the freezer chest rocked as something slammed into the outside of it. I heard a couple of grunts.

Then I swore I heard Iz's voice.

"Quick—get his handcuffs on him," she said.

Maybe I was hallucinating. Or maybe he had shot me dead after all, but my ghost was too stupid to know that the final bell had just rung.

And then for the second time in a week, I was looking up from the bottom of a freezer chest at Iz's and Kenny's faces.

We stayed frozen like that for a minute, until Kenny said, "Dude, we surrender. Don't shoot."

I lowered the gun. Iz reached down and touched my cheek. "Are you okay?" Her voice had gone helium high.

I wasn't actually sure I was okay, but nodding seemed like the right thing to do. "Except I think I busted my ankle. You're going to have to help me get out," I said to Kenny. I handed the gun and the flashlight up to Iz, who put them somewhere.

Kenny leaned over and got his hands under my armpits. Somehow he managed to hoist me over the side. Then, between the two of them, they got me seated against a pile of garbage a few feet away.

Iz immediately started fluttering around me, murmuring and poking at the various places on my anatomy that probably should have hurt. I guess I was lucky; right then everything was just numb.

"I'm okay." Maybe if I just kept saying it, it would come true. I finally grabbed one of her hands and pulled her down next to me. I figured if I didn't stop her soon, she was going to pull out that mother trick of spitting into a Kleenex and washing my face with it. Besides, I needed something to hang on to. My head was spinning like the time Kalooky had beaned me with a baseball.

Iz had set the flashlight on the ground. In its beam I could see Deputy Death lying on his stomach. His eyes were closed. His hands were handcuffed behind him. Kenny was now sitting on his legs.

I looked over at Kenny. "Hey. Touché. What did you two do to him?"

Kenny pointed at another flashlight on the ground. This one was even bigger than Gram's. The glass was broken.

Iz answered. "We got up as close as we dared, and Kenny threw his dad's flashlight at him. Hit him square on the back of the head. All that football stuff finally paid off."

"Iz thought of it. We heard him threatening you and saying all that junk about hurting your grandma, and then he talked about the flashlight your dad had dropped, and next thing I knew, Iz was whispering in my ear what I had to do. He went down like I dropped him with my dad's .22. I wasn't actually sure it would work that well."

Once Kenny started talking, his words came out way too fast. I gave him a closer look. Even in the flashlight beam, he was the approximate color of one of Crazy Carl's little green men. Then suddenly he jumped up, leaned over into the freezer chest, and puked his guts out. I was glad I wasn't still inside.

Iz and I looked away to give him some privacy. When he came up for air, he sat down on Deputy Death again. Maybe it was comfortable — who knew?

"But before that, how did you even get here?" I said.

Iz poked me in the side, hard. "I couldn't believe how stupid you were being, so I woke up Kenny and we followed you. There's this great shortcut through the Theilmann farm, so we got here pretty fast. We were just pulling up to the fence when we saw the deputy's car coming, so we hid out while we tried to figure out exactly what was going on."

Kenny broke in. "We could hear you guys from where we were hiding. When he started admitting some of the stuff he'd done, we weren't sure what to do. Iz got this idea that we should create a diversion so you could run, but then those raccoons started fighting and did it for us."

I interrupted. "You mean that screaming—those were raccoons? I thought maybe it was Carl. It sounded like a crazy person—or like somebody getting murdered."

Iz shivered. "The deputy was so focused on finding you that he didn't notice us stalking him. So when we finally saw our chance with the flashlight, we took it."

"But what are we gonna do now? We can't call 911. He *is* 911. We can't call him." Kenny was babbling again.

"Kenny!" said Iz. "Don't make me slap you with my flip-flop."

He took a deep breath. It seemed to steady him some. "I gotta call my dad. He is *so* gonna kill me, but I don't know what else to do. Do you have your cell?"

I felt my mouth drop open.

"What?" Iz said.

"It's in the freezer. Back corner. I hope you didn't hurl on it, bro."

Kenny got up again and fished the phone out of the freezer. It appeared to be dry.

"Let me have it for a minute," I said.

I took it from him and turned off the recorder. Then I hit Rewind for just a second and then Play.

"For a minute," my voice echoed back at me, loud and clear.

Iz and Kenny were both staring.

"Be careful with it," I said, giving it back to Kenny. "I think I got enough on record here to hang him high."

Kenny took the phone as if I had handed him a poisonous snake. I didn't know if it was because of my warning or because he was that afraid of calling his dad. His hands were shaking. Seeing them made me realize I was shaking too. Not to mention that I was wishing for the good old days when I had felt completely numb. Every pulse of my blood was starting to feel like a heavy-metal drummer was crashing down on my ankle with his drumsticks.

"How do you dial this stupid thing?" Kenny asked. Iz took it and punched in a number. But she must have been a little nervous too, because she had somehow hit Speakerphone and we could all hear it ringing through. One. Two. She handed the phone back to Kenny as Big Ken's sleepy voice cut off the third ring.

"Hello?"

"Dad, it's me." Kenny stopped and swallowed real big.

"Kenny?" Big Ken sounded completely confused, and we could hear somebody in the background—Jen, I guessed—mumble something.

Then his voice got more alert. "Kenny, where are you? It's the middle of the night."

"Dad, listen. You know how you said that I could call you anytime for help, no matter what trouble I was in, and you'd come right away and not yell until later?"

"What's wrong? Are you hurt? Where are you?" Big Ken sounded wide awake now, and there were excited noises from Jen in the background.

"No, Dad, I'm okay—just listen, all right? Me and Trav and Iz, we're out at the dump, and we need you to come. To the dump. Right away. And help us."

"Kenny! You swear you're okay?" We could hear all sorts of rustling coming from Big Ken's end of the phone now, and then it sounded as if he'd dropped the receiver altogether, because it banged on something. I didn't know what he was doing—maybe getting dressed.

"Dad!"

"All right, it's going to be okay. I'm leaving right now. Kenny, I want you to hang up this line and call me back on my cell if you need me before I can get there."

"Hurry, Dad." Kenny clicked off and handed the phone back to Iz. "He is *so* going to kill me," he said, staring off into space.

I hadn't exactly gotten the impression that Big Ken was racing out to the dump to strangle Kenny. I guess there were ways to interpret dad-speak that Kenny understood and I didn't. And maybe he'd seen some of the same shows I had; Animal Planet was always featuring animal fathers who killed their own offspring.

Iz brought the phone back and sat down close beside me. She probably could tell I was still shaking like Jell-O at a fundraiser, because she pretty quickly leaned in closer and wrapped her arm around my back.

"I can't believe he was really going to shoot you for that money," she said.

At the word "money," my head jerked up. Iz looked at me.

"I know where it is," I blurted out.

Kenny looked over too. "Dude?"

"I mean, I think I know. But it all fits. It explains everything. It was right over there. I remember the mannequin. We're just ten feet away."

Kenny and Iz were both staring at me as if I had transformed into one of the voices inside Crazy Carl's head. I wanted to pound on my ankle in frustration, but even I'm not that stupid.

"Just take the flashlight and go around to the other side of this mound and look. It's only been a few days. A holiday weekend. They can't be buried too deep."

"Bro, look, Dad will be here soon and we'll get you to the hospital—"

"No, listen—remember that morning you found me down in Gram's cellar?" They both nodded.

"I was cleaning her old freezer chest. I emptied out all these really old packages. They were labeled like they were fish and deer and stuff my dad had hunted. Carl saw me dump them right there behind that mound. Iz, you said yourself that he goes through all the junk here to see what he can sell off. The day after Gram and I hauled the bags out here, Carl was in town spending all this money. The same day they found the bait money. I just figured it all out, right before you took down the deputy. My dad hid the money in Gram's freezer fourteen years ago, and it sat there until I got to Minnesota and hauled it here to the dump."

Kenny jumped to his feet and picked up the flashlight. "The other side of this mound? What do these packages look like?"

"They're in those pumpkin leaf bags from Halloween, you know? They're bright orange—you can't miss them."

Kenny disappeared around the mound but Iz stayed where she was. I felt her arm tighten around my back. Her voice came out low so that I had to lean even closer to hear her. "When I heard those raccoons screaming, for a minute I thought it was you. I thought he'd hurt you. I thought somebody else was going to be . . . just gone from my life."

Hearing that, I felt so crappy that I had to look away. "I'm sorry. You were right. Again. Coming out here on my own at night was stupid. Maybe next time I'll actually listen to you."

She gave a little sniff. I couldn't tell if it was a "fat chance" sniff or if she was starting to cry, so I finally turned my head in her direction.

And then somehow we were kissing, and it turned out that kissing is one of those things that goes much better once you stop thinking so much and just do it. Because as soon as we did, everything kind of worked itself out. It was like how I always imagined flying might be: head-rushing, gut-leaping, my pulse jumping double time when she curled her arm around my neck.

"Iz!" Kenny's voice boomed over the mound. "Get over here and help me look!"

Iz pulled back slowly and we looked at each other for another heart thump. Then she stood up, pulled another flashlight out of her pocket, and turned it on. She looked from me to where Deputy Death still lay stretched on the ground.

I could tell what she was thinking. "I'll keep the flashlight but you go help Kenny," I said. "You'll only be ten feet away."

I lit her way around the mound. "If he moves one muscle, you start yelling," she said.

Actually, screaming was starting to sound like a good idea; without Iz to lean on, I was feeling a little shaky again. Pain was beginning to slice and burn my ankle into strips of beef jerky. I was pretty sure that if it kept getting worse, before long I'd be begging Kenny to just shoot me after all.

I turned the flashlight directly onto Deputy Death and discovered his eyes glittering in the light. He seemed to be staring straight at me.

I tried to focus in on everything he'd told me, but my brain skittered away from grasping all of it. It was like when you try to push together the same poles of two different magnets; hard as you try to force them, they repel. Hard as I pushed, my mind couldn't seem to keep hold of the fact that the deputy had killed my father.

"Did you really kill him?" I said. "I thought he used to be your friend."

He didn't answer. It was probably a good thing that I didn't know where Iz had put his gun.

Then Kenny and Iz walked back around the mound. Iz dropped an orange bag with a jack-o'-lantern face at my feet and sat down next to me again.

Kenny returned to his seat on Deputy Death's legs. "Right where you said it would be, man. Didn't even have to dig too far for it."

I ripped open the bag and pulled out a white-wrapped package. "Walleye," it said, in handwriting I now recognized. I unwound the white paper.

It wasn't poor Nemo.

The package was crammed full of crisp twenties. The old-fashioned kind. It had to be the cash my father had used to buy his own death.

I held up a handful for Kenny and Iz to see. And Deputy Death went crazy.

He let out this wolf howl and somehow kicked up with his legs. Kenny had been staring at me and the money. The whole bucking-bronco thing took him by complete surprise and he went rolling.

Fortunately, Kenny lives and breathes to give people the chance to try to crush him. His football reflexes got him out of the way of those killer boots just in time.

Which was how he happened to be pinning down Deputy Death with the freezer chest just as Big Ken rounded the corner.

At first it looked like maybe Kenny and Animal Planet were onto something. Big Ken swung all 180 or so pounds of his only son up and off the ground in what was either a crushing hug or some kind of extended strangulation ritual. It was actually a pretty impressive show of strength for a guy his age. I would have been worried except Kenny seemed to be holding his own, hugging him back.

Eventually Big Ken let go of Kenny and crouched

down in front of me and Iz. He hugged her, too, and then took her chin in his hand and gave her a long once-over. Then he turned to me.

"I'm good, man," I said. I put up my hands, palms out. I didn't think I had enough air left in me to survive one of his death grips. "Thanks for coming."

He spotted my ankle, which had swollen up to softball size, and before I could say anything else, he'd reached out to touch it. My whole body convulsed as if he'd zapped me with lightning.

"Okay." He reached out again and gently leaned me back up against Iz. "I'm sorry. I know it hurts. I had to find out if your foot was still getting blood flow. But it's not turning cold. Now try to wiggle your toes for me. Good? We'll get you to a doctor. You'll be okay."

It was nice to know somebody thought so. I was actually pretty sure I was going to hurl in Iz's lap.

I'd forgotten about the money. I had thrown it into the air when Big Ken had touched my ankle and I'd jumped like that. A little breeze picked up a couple of the bills and they fluttered like moths in the light. Big Ken turned his head and watched them float away.

Then he stood up and looked at the freezer chest.

A steady stream of wash-your-mouth-out-with-soap vocabulary words were pouring out from underneath it.

"I'm almost afraid to confirm this, but who do you have trapped under there, Kenny?"

"It's Deputy Anderson. Dad, you're not going to believe this—he admitted he was in on that bank robbery, and he said he killed Trav's dad, too. He wanted the money real bad. He was going to shoot Trav to get it, and maybe hurt his grandma. So it's a really good thing we followed Trav out here, right, because we, like, saved his life? By hitting the deputy with your big flashlight. Sorry it's broken. We didn't have a choice, Dad—the deputy's some way heinous dude."

Big Ken kind of scrubbed at his face with his hands. Then I think he borrowed one of Deputy Death's vocabulary words, but he said it behind his hands, so I wasn't positive.

"I'm going to nutshell this, Kenny, to make sure I understand correctly. On a day when you'd already been grounded for fighting, you and your cousin left the house in the middle of the night, without permission and without asking an adult for help, to come out to the dump. You discovered an officer of the law confessing to serious crimes and threatening someone with his gun, so you confronted him with only my flashlight as a weapon? Which, by the way, is now broken?"

"I guess that's one way to put it," said Kenny.

"Okay, I just wanted to make sure I had everything clear." Big Ken scrubbed at his face once more. "All right. First you and I are going to pull this freezer off the deputy."

"But, Dad—"

"Kenny, I think we've already got enough to deal with, without you being hauled in for smothering him. Does he still have his gun?"

"Here it is, Uncle Ken." Iz got up and pulled it out of a door-less refrigerator. Once they'd hoisted up the freezer chest, Big Ken took the gun from her and stood looking down at Deputy Death for a moment. The deputy shut up pretty quickly. I think I might have, too, if I'd had Big Ken giving me that look with a gun in his hand.

"All right, I want you two to very carefully elevate Travis's ankle. Put that bag of trash under it." He pointed to the pumpkin bag. My injured ankle was going to be resting on the most expensive footstool any of us would ever see.

Big Ken pulled out his cell. "After that, you all stay perfectly still until I'm done calling the people who need to be called. But"—and he pointed the phone at Kenny—"please don't assume we're finished discussing this whole episode. By the time we're done with it, you're going to wish for the good old days when being grounded was your biggest problem." He started dialing one-handedly, never taking his eyes or the gun off Deputy Death.

"See? I told you! He is *so* going to kill me." Kenny's shoulders slumped.

Like I said, that was the Animal Planet view too. But seriously, wasn't that how I ended up in this whole mess—listening to them about the wack walking catfish?

Maybe it was time I switched channels.

CHAPTER 26

I know you're excited to be out of that cast. But remember what the doctor said. I don't want you to hurt yourself again."

"Huh?" I'd been staring at the freak show also known as the bottom half of my right leg since we'd left the specialist. After six weeks it had emerged from the cast fish-belly white and withered. And a little stinky, too.

"Have you been listening to me at all?"

Okay, it was time for me to switch my focus. After all, Ma and I had a new deal in place now.

"I promise to be careful, Mommy. No more running away from killers. I'll just stand still and let the next one catch me so I don't break my ankle again."

"Ha!" She took a hand off the steering wheel and

reached over to squeeze my arm. "There's my favorite smart aleck. These past few weeks I've kind of wondered where he was."

I glanced over at her. "Still here. I just wasn't sure that was the kid you wanted."

"I'll take whatever kid I can get, especially if he's in one piece." She clicked off the car radio and together we listened to the silence for a minute. "But I'll let you in on a little secret, kiddo. I'll take my smart aleck any day over the Travis I found when I first walked into that hospital room. That Trav had me scared. I'm still pretty worried about you."

"Hey, Ma, cut a guy some slack. I don't know how you got to Minnesota as fast as you did, but even so, by the time you showed up, they'd already put me through a medieval torture ritual in the ER. Plus, I think every cop from the FBI to who knows—the Secret Service and the KGB, maybe—had thumbscrewed me to get all the gory details. Seeing you after all that just . . . surprised me. I think I'd earned the right to a tiny little breakdown at that point."

She took enough time out of driving to give me the classic Mother Look.

"And now? How are you feeling now? You have to

be honest with me, Trav. This is important. Because I won't leave today if you need me to stay longer."

I looked out the window of her rental while I thought about it. High over the cornfields a flocking spiral of giant birds were funneling up into the sky like a white tornado. Gram had told me they were pelicans, riding the thermals so they could fly as high as possible without wasting any energy. Birds, man—they have life all figured out.

Then I recognized the cornfields: we were almost back to Gram's house. My house too, at least for now.

"Really, Ma, I'm back to all good. Better than I've been in a long time. I swear. Now that people have quit staring at me like I'm some kind of circus act, it really is better. Even that shrink doc has been helping. It's the right thing for you to go back to California."

"Even though I'm not at all sure it's the right thing for me to let you stay in Minnesota." My mom sighed.

"I'm gonna be okay. We're gonna be okay. The shrink doc says there are a lot of different ways to make a family work. And you and Dale—that's good for you. I get that. But I need to be here right now. You letting me stay with Gram is huge for me."

"It's pretty huge for me too, Trav. So remember:

I'm not agreeing to a permanent change. We're going to keep talking about it. Maybe every single night during those Skype calls you've agreed to. I'm kind of counting on the fact that once it starts to get cold here, you'll race back home. And when you're ready to give him a chance, you're going to find out that Dale really is a good guy."

I nodded because I knew she needed me to. Then she pulled the car into Gram's driveway and we both climbed out. My right leg felt a little shaky, like it was still going to be a while before I could count on the ground feeling solid underneath me. But it was good to be out from under the weight of that cast.

"It took longer at the doctor than I expected, so I'm glad I packed the rental before we left," Ma said. "I've got to dash if I'm going to make my plane. I said goodbye to your grandma earlier, so all that's left now is a hug from you that has to last me until Dale and I come visit in October."

I'd had lots of opportunities to work on my hugging lately; I was getting pretty good at it.

Ma stepped back but she left her hands on my shoulders. "So tall. I swear I'll tell your Gram to stop feeding you if you keep this up behind my back." She dropped her hands and looked down at her feet for a minute. Then she looked back at me.

"Travis . . . it's a hard thing to have to admit to your kid that you didn't know his father as well as you should have, all things considered. But along with all the other stories you've heard, I want you to remember that the guy I met when I got that job here after college was sweet and funny and smart. He was a lot of good things. I just didn't think he was ready to be a good father."

I gave her another hug. "I love you, Ma."

When I walked into the house after my mom had driven away, Gram was watching out the window. "She misses you already, you know."

I nodded and headed for the fridge.

"Travis." Gram's voice had changed; I looked over and felt a kick in my gut. Her face had this pinched look; I'd seen it often enough over the past weeks to know it meant bad news.

"I had a call this morning from the sheriff's office. They've confirmed that the body they dug up at the Anderson farm was your father."

I hated seeing that look on her face again. "But that's good, isn't it? Now it doesn't matter if parts of my cell-phone recording were garbled or that me and Kenny and Iz are only kids and the jury might not believe us. Finding the body buried on the deputy's family farm pretty much means they can hang him high, right?"

Of course, there was other evidence against him too. Like the fact that he'd never actually called in the FBI—I mean, he wanted the money himself, and he couldn't risk getting the Feds reinvolved in the case. And there was the receipt they found in his house for the tracking device he'd planted under my bike seat. And the newspaper he'd used to cut out letters for the anonymous note—dude, note to self: *recycling doesn't always pay.*

But Gram didn't respond when I said that about hanging him high, so I figured I'd gone too far. "Sorry," I said.

She shook her head. "No, I understand why you're so angry at him. I just thought the news might make it all . . . too real for you."

It had actually felt pretty real to me back when

I'd been staring up at a gun from the bottom of the freezer chest. But Gram hadn't been sleeping much since they'd dug up that body; I think it was the thing that had made it all too real for her.

"Maybe . . . I'm hoping maybe now it will start to feel like something in the past and we can move on to other stuff, you know?" I said. "I mean, school starts in just a couple weeks. I gotta get my head clear for that or I'm dead meat as the new kid all over again."

"Are you still having those nightmares?"

"They don't bother me so much anymore." It was only a sideways lie. Gram spent enough of her time worrying over me; I didn't want her to know that I still had a bad night once in a while. But I had figured out a trick to get myself back to sleep faster. I'd given Linnea a little plastic bottle and bribed her to smuggle me some of Iz's strawberry shampoo. One little sniff and the bad dreams faded fast.

"If you can stand to wait a while for lunch, I've got something in mind I'd like to do first. Will you run next door and ask Kenny if we can borrow his boat?" Gram's face had relaxed; now she just looked tired.

"Sure. Okay." I didn't have a clue as to why we

were planning a cruise, but I started limping next door to see if Kenny was back yet from football practice. Then my cell phone pinged.

The text read, "The Big Kalook is finally home. I ninja-ed my last grizzly. Have u died from boredom yet at step-pa's house?"

I texted back, "Died from boredom? No. Psycho killer? Close call. Will fill u in l8r."

Linnea answered the door at Kenny's house. "You're home from the doctor! Want to play?"

Somehow I'd become a seven-year-old's BFF. Iz had decided to work her way back onto the swim team, so Linnea and I had logged a lot of lifeguard duty together on the dock. Turns out the squid is a total card shark; I'd lost something like a hundred forty-nine Tootsie Pops to her in Go Fish.

Kenny waved a sandwich at me when I limped into his house. "Dude! What did the doctor say about football?"

"Dude." I shook my head and sighed in fake sorrow. "No go. He says the ankle's looking pretty good but I can't risk a contact sport."

Kenny looked totally deflated. For weeks now,

he'd been telling anyone who'd listen how football had saved my life. And the funniest part was that the *Prairie Press* had run with that angle. The headline had read: "Future All-Star Throws Lifesaver Pass." Iz told me Jen bought ten copies and sent them to all the relatives.

So Kenny was convinced that I'd want to return football the favor of saving my butt by risking a broken neck alongside him every week. But I was way relieved when the bone doc confirmed I shouldn't be doing anything that involved facing down mutants like Cody Svengrud for "fun."

Kenny turned on that high-wattage grin of his. "Check this out." He pulled a new cell phone out of his pocket and lowered his voice. "I've officially finished serving out the terms of my prison sentence, so Dad let me get this. He made me put the rest of my reward money into a college fund, but he said he figured I better have a cell handy so I could call him the next time I decide to be an idiot." Kenny gave me a look. "You sure you're not second-guessing giving all that cash to me and Iz, man?"

I shook my head. I'd never forget what Gram had

said about the robbery money doing damage to our family. No way I wanted to be the one to extend that curse; Iz and Kenny were welcome to the reward.

Kenny was cool with Gram's plan to borrow his boat, but between my wimpy leg and Gram's limpy one, it took a while for him to load the two of us safely inside. Then Gram had to wave off his elaborate instructions about how to run the motor.

"Thank you, Kenny. I may be an old lady but I've lived on this lake all my life. This isn't my first time piloting a boat. We'll be fine."

Sure enough, she had us skimming across the water in no time. We bypassed the island and bounced out to the middle of the lake before she let the motor die. The surface had been mirror-still back at shore, but out here sudden spits of a fickle breeze were kicking up small waves in all different directions. We drifted, rocking slightly from side to side. I tried to ignore my aching leg while I waited for Gram to tell me what was going on. She talked a lot more than she used to, but it still seemed to take her longer than most people to get started. I'd learned it was better to just let her come to things at her own speed.

Finally she leaned over and picked up a plastic bag she'd thrown onto the floor of the boat. Then she looked at me. "Your father always loved the water. And since that day they came to tell me he was missing, I've always thought of him as being out here . . . somewhere. I would stand and look out over the lake and even talk to him sometimes."

Gram went quiet again, shading her eyes and staring out over the expanse of sun-diamonded lake. The steamy air was thick enough to have drops of sweat slicking down my neck. In moments like that, it was hard to buy everybody's warnings about how frozen I'd feel in just a couple of months. But I guess it was true that winter comes early to Minnesota.

Gram turned her eyes to me again. "I suppose it sounds morbid, me picturing him out here. Or fanciful. But it helped me to think of him somewhere, other than just gone without a trace. When they first dug up that body and told me it was probably John . . . I suppose I should have been relieved they'd found him. But I felt like I'd lost my son all over again. So this morning I decided I should bring him back out here."

I gotta admit, my eyes were now glued to that plastic bag.

She reached inside. And pulled out that lumpy fish key-holder thing my father had made her in shop class. She stared at it a moment, then closed her eyes. I saw her lips move. Then she curled it in toward her body and Frisbeed it back out across the water.

She had quite an arm for an old lady. The wooden fish sailed high through the air and then skimmed across two waves like a skipping stone. Then it slipped down into the water, popping up almost immediately to bounce along the waves. Every time it rocked toward the sun, it sent a light beam flashing back to the sky.

I wasn't sure what to say, but I figured I had to contribute something. A prayer, maybe? Except I really knew only one by heart, and reciting that line "if I should die before I wake" didn't seem like the right thing to do in that moment. So something else—something really sensitive and profound?

"I expected it to sink, but it looks like it's staying afloat," I said.

So one thing hadn't changed: I was still completely clueless.

But Gram seemed pretty pleased with that. This little smile curved her lips in a way I hadn't seen in a while, and she gave a short nod. "You're exactly right, Travis; sometimes not sinking is a pretty good thing. I'm going to stay focused on just that." She started the motor and clutched the side of the boat. "Hang on, boy—I want to show you what we used to call a boat ride."

I turned around to face forward and grabbed the side as the boat jerked into motion. Gulls scattered into the air like bowling pins as we cut across the water at high speed. I gripped harder and leaned into the cool spitting spray so it would soak my sweaty T-shirt.

Gram slowed down when we finished curving around the island. I wiped the water out of my eyes so that I had a clear view of the shore. Somebody was waiting for us on Kenny's dock. As we drew closer, the figure grew bigger; when it suddenly transformed into Iz, all my nerve endings short-circuited the way they always did when I first saw her for the day. A few yards out, Gram cut the motor altogether, and we slowed to a glide, momentum carrying us in until we bumped up against the dock pole. Then Iz leaned out over the water and grabbed my hand, and together we guided the boat the last few feet home.

Acknowledgments

Minnesota has 11,842 lakes, give or take, but my particular lake—with the rundown cabin my extended family has crowded into since my mother was a girl—is Green Lake, near the towns of Spicer and New London. All of the good reasons that make Trav want to stay in Minnesota come from my love for that small corner of the universe. But the lake in this story is not that specific lake, and the town in this story is not either of those specific towns; if you're ever fortunate enough to visit my Green Lake, you won't find an island, or a giant statue of a bullhead, or anyone behaving as badly as some of the people Trav meets. In fact, you won't find the actual people and events that I describe, because I made them up for the sake of my story. (Except that there really are butter heads at the Minnesota State Fair, and according to news reports, they do make their way to freezers across the state.)

I have many amazing people in my life; I couldn't possibly thank all of them here. But several of them played a role in helping me with this book. My thanks go to:

Editor Adah Nuchi, whose editorial work was so adept, and done in such expert sleight-of-hand fashion that readers might be left with the mistaken conclusion that

I deserve more of the credit than I do for the shaping of this story.

Everyone else on the Houghton Mifflin Harcourt team who played a role in bringing this book to life and helping it find an audience. I entrusted you with my story, and I am enormously proud to be able to share the beautiful book you created with readers.

Agent Rubin Pfeffer, the most gracious person I've met in my twenty-seven years of working in the world of books. I am more than fortunate that you took a chance on me.

Vicki and Steve Palmquist, the extraordinary founders of Children's Literature Network, who are untiring in their support of me and unequaled in their support of the worldwide network of all those who bring books and kids together. My world would be much smaller without you.

Author/illustrator/hero Debra Frasier, who did me a momentous favor. I know that I am not the first to benefit from her bigheartedness, or to find that her favors hold their own kind of magic.

Mystery writer Ellen Hart, an exceptional and generous writing teacher. The feedback and encouragement from Ellen and my fellow students carried me through the hardest part of writing this story. Diane Ferreira, Sue McCauley, and Lindsay Nielsen in particular provided valuable additional advice.

Writing group members Stephanie Weller Hanson, Wendy Rubinyi, and Patricia McKernon Runkle, who always knew whether I most needed a kick or a hug.

Aimée Bissonette, Mary Cummings, Donna Gephart, Marsha Qualey, and Laura Purdie Salas, who offered an equally valuable mix of professional expertise and friendly support.

Creative coach Rosanne Bane, who always knows both the right thing—and the write thing—to say.

Joy Baker, Jim Bullard, Joel Bullard, Sam Bullard, Lee Engfer, Therese Naber, Erik Rubinyi, Maxwell Schander, Roberta Steele, and Katherine Werner, who offered their wise insights as early manuscript readers or encouragers.

The extended Bengtson/LaPatka family, who truly are the best neighbors ever, and who have had a hand in shaping some of my favorite Lake memories.

The family members and friends who have filled me with love and laughter, and who allow me to steal their stories and make them my own. See you next summer at the Lake!